SEE NO EVIL

JUSTICE AGAIN
BOOK SIX

M A COMLEY

To Michele, thank you for allowing me to use your name in this book and for all you do for me, daily. Forever grateful, dear friend.

ACKNOWLEDGMENTS

Special thanks as always go to @studioenp for their superb cover design expertise.

My heartfelt thanks go to my wonderful editor Emmy, and my proofreader Joseph for spotting all the lingering nits.

Thank you also to my amazing ARC Group who help to keep me sane during this process.

To Mary, gone, but never forgotten. I hope you found the peace you were searching for my dear friend. I miss you each and every day.

ALSO BY M A COMLEY

Clever Deception (co-written by Linda S Prather)

Tragic Deception (co-written by Linda S Prather)

Sinful Deception (co-written by Linda S Prather)

PROLOGUE

The night was getting chilly, only to be expected at this time of year. They'd recently had a few snow flurries in this part of the world, unusual for London, but they couldn't complain. Overall, the winter had been pretty kind to them. However, Paula was looking forward to the following month, March. Her birthday was in the first week, and her husband, Adrian, had promised to take her away to Paris for the weekend. Now that was really something to look forward to, in her eyes.

At twenty-six, Paula was the oldest member of the group, in her class even, but going back to university was something she had always planned to do at some stage. Adrian had been a huge support when she had first approached him about giving up her secretarial career to study psychology, but that enthusiasm had dwindled somewhat lately, once the cost-of-living crisis had struck. Now the onus of paying for the huge spike in bills lay firmly around his shoulders, and on a mechanic's paltry salary, they were struggling.

The thought of going home and getting into yet another

row made her shudder. She pulled the collar of her coat up around her neck.

"Are you all right, Paula?" Tina asked.

She was such a sweet girl. The most attentive of students who soaked up all the information going during every lecture they attended, whereas Paula was often guilty of drifting off, her mind, more often than not, dwelling on the minus figure in her bank account.

"I'm okay. Just feeling guilty again, you know why."

"I do. You and Adrian will come through this rough patch, hon. I have all my fingers and toes crossed for you. Are you still going away for your birthday?"

Paula's mouth twisted. "I hope so. It depends if we can spare the cash. It's not looking likely, although I'm trying to think positively."

"That's my girl. Negativity, when it festers, can do a lot of damage up here." Tina tapped her temple. "I should know, I used to let it interfere with my life until a couple of years ago. I gave myself a good talking-to and set out to turn my life around."

"I need to find out how I can do that, search for something that will work on me. I tried doing yoga, like you suggested, but it's so difficult when Adrian comes home from work and wants to talk about his day."

"I get that. Hey, you should be grateful, most girls I know say their fellas ignore them most of the time in the evening. Either they're down the pub drinking or they're stuck on their game consoles with their mates."

"I suppose, maybe it's because we're married and both take our roles seriously, compared to just going out with each other."

They paused and knocked their cans of lager together and then necked half of the contents.

"I should be going soon. Mum was expecting me home

early. She wanted me to look after my sister while she went to her evening class." Tina glanced at her watch and bounced to her feet. "Shit, I'd totally forgotten about it until then. I must dash. See you in class in the morning."

"Take care walking home. Do you want me to come with you?"

"I'll be legging it home, and no, you stay here and enjoy yourself with the others." Tina bent down and pecked her on the cheek.

"Hope you don't get into too much bother for being late, hon."

Tina waved and called out a 'see you' to the other members of the group and left the top of the building.

Yes, they were in their usual hangout, on the roof of one of the campus buildings. One of the boys had managed to obtain a key for the off-limits zone. They weren't doing any harm, they came here frequently, after class had ended, just to wind down over a few bevvies. With money so tight, Paula knew she was in the wrong, but wasn't that what university was all about? Busting your balls in class only to let your hair down with your mates afterwards? That's how she had justified the situation.

She rubbed her hands together, feeling the nip in the air even more now. A couple of the girls had already begun to drift off. There were six of the group left. Although she wanted to head home, she always held back from being one of the first to leave, her insecurity showing. Her rationale was that if she did that, the group might stop asking her to tag along with them.

Boris came up and sat beside her. "How's it going, Paula? You did well answering that tricky question in class today."

Her cheeks warmed up. "You think so? I thought the answer was a logical one. I was shocked no one else came up

3

with a solution. I'm fine, same old, same old. How is it going with you? Are you enjoying the course?"

"It's getting better. I wasn't too sure in the beginning, but now things have settled down at home and the pressure is off there, I suppose it's given me more headspace to concentrate on my studies."

"I'm sorry you're going through a tough time. Do you want to talk about it?"

He shrugged. "Not right now. Up here, this is our fun time, isn't it? It's not supposed to be about the doom and gloom of our ordinary lives, is it?"

"I guess. I'm always around if you need a shoulder to cry on, just ask, okay?"

"Thanks, I'll bear it in mind."

Her mobile tinkled in her coat pocket; she'd forgotten to put it on vibrate. She removed it to find Adrian's name on the caller ID screen. She sighed and mumbled, "Here we go, it's him indoors, ready to have another go at me, no doubt."

Boris took the hint and left her to it. "See you later."

She smiled and mouthed thanks then answered the call. "Hi, Adrian. Are you at home yet?"

"I am and I expected to find you here. What's going on, Paula? I left for work at seven-thirty this morning and I've just got home now at six-thirty to find the house empty."

"In other words, you anticipated me being there with your dinner ready and waiting on the table, right?"

"Is it too much to ask? You do very little else during the day anyway."

Paula swallowed down the lump threatening to lodge in her throat and rolled her eyes up to the clear black sky above, the stars twinkling and the half-moon bright, not a cloud in sight. "I'm going to ignore that dig. I'm on my way now. I had to stay behind and see one of my lecturers about my coursework. That's what we students have to do, occasionally, you know."

"Whoopie do! And there's me, stuck here all alone with just the cat to keep me company. She's starving as well. What's for dinner tonight?"

"I haven't got the foggiest. I suggest you see if there's anything lurking in the freezer because the fridge is as empty as my bank account."

"Shit! Are you telling me you haven't been shopping all week?"

"Yep. Have you? You eat your weight in food every week. I'm just as busy as you are. Where does it say in the Marriage Handbook that doing the shopping is always down to the female in the relationship?"

"Sod off. Don't start this again. You women fought for equality all those years ago. I've got news for you, I go to work every day as my share of the bargain, the least you can do is be here to feed me when I get home at night."

"Your meaning of equality and mine are vastly different. I'm not going there, not over the phone, Adrian. I'll be home soon enough, we can thrash it out then."

"Thrash it out? Is that what our marriage has descended to, thrashing things out rather than debating them and working around the issue in a peaceful way?"

"It sounds like it, judging by the tone of your voice."

The others drifted off during her conversation. She appreciated them not hanging around to listen to her side of the argument.

"See you over at the pub, for a quickie," Heidi whispered.

Paula shook her head and pointed at the phone. She covered the mouthpiece and said, "I'd better leave it tonight."

"Okay, no problem. See you in the morning. Hope you get things sorted out."

Paula gave a thumbs-up and continued her conversation with her husband.

"What does that mean?" Adrian asked.

"I'm tired. I'll be home within twenty minutes, we'll discuss it further, or maybe we won't, when I get there."

"That's your answer to everything, isn't it? Brush it all under the carpet, ignore the problems in the hope they will drift away. Not this time, Paula. You and I need to sit down and have a frank and open discussion once and for all, if we want this marriage to work."

"Is that some kind of threat?" When she glanced around her, she found she was all alone up on the roof. She shuddered at the thought of being in the open space by herself.

"No, not really. Come on, Paula, you know as well as I do, marriage is supposed to be give and take. At the moment, it seems like I'm the one always giving and you're the one always taking."

Tears burned her eyes. "Bollocks, is it fuck! How dare you say that? I work just as hard as you during the day."

"Do you? I've seen your schedule, you have dozens of free periods, and yet this house is a tip. Why can't you come home during the day and tidy up, or better still, go to the supermarket and stock up the cupboards?"

"I'm not going there. I'm hanging up now. We'll continue this when I get home."

"Whatever." Adrian beat her to it by ending the call first.

Irate, she leaned her head back against the wall and wondered, not for the first time, in which direction her life was going. She thought enrolling in university would be the making of her and their marriage. Instead, it appeared to be ripping it to shreds. Maybe she should consider what the consequences would be if she continued. This was supposed to be the answer to their prayers, putting in the graft now to give her, *give them*, a better future with a superior income to what Adrian was likely to bring in as a mechanic. This was all about making their future a brighter one than it had been if she had continued in her secretarial role. She had grand ideas of starting up her own business, offering counselling to those in need, guiding them through life's traumas and seeing them through the other side of their dilemmas.

A noise alerted her, tearing her out of her self-pitying mode. The door swung in the breeze. Relieved, she bent down to collect her bag and stood. With her lager can in one hand and her phone in the other, she moved towards the door, only to see it slam shut in front of her. A figure stood there, a balaclava disguising the person's face.

"Who are you? What do you want?" she asked, her voice faltering severely, the fear increasing.

"I've come to collect what you owe me." The person was definitely a male.

Confused, Paula shook her head. "You've got the wrong person. I don't owe you anything."

"Oh, but you do. Give me your phone." He held out his hand.

Paula clutched her prized possession to her chest. "I refuse to. It's my lifeline. Without it, I'm lost."

He took a step forward and slapped her around the face. "Give it to me or what I have planned for you is going to be a whole lot worse, you can take my word for that."

"No. Don't make me hand it over."

Another slap sent her head jerking to the right, her neck clicking noisily in objection. "Why? Why do you want it?"

"You'll see soon enough. Hand it over, now." He removed something long from the inside of his jacket.

Paula gasped when the blade glinted in the moonlight. "No, you don't have to do this. Here, take it. You can have my phone, just leave me alone, please." She handed over the mobile.

He paused before taking it. "Unlock it."

"What? Why?"

"Do it," He ordered, the blade inching towards her chest.

Her hand shook. It took three attempts to unlock the phone. She handed it back.

He scrolled through it and then began typing. Every few seconds, his gaze flitted between her and the phone.

I need to get out of here. She eyed the door, but he was standing too close to it, blocking her escape route.

"There, all done. We can get down to business now."

"What are you talking about? I want to go home. My husband is expecting me."

He laughed, tipping his head back. "That's what you think."

"Give me the phone. What have you done?"

He laughed again and jabbed the knife towards her throat. "I'm the one in charge around here, not you."

"All right. There's no need for you to get angry with me. What do you want from me? I don't have any money, I'm a student, riddled with debt."

"If you're searching for pity, don't bother. Step backwards, nice and slowly, away from the door."

"Why?"

The knife came to within a few inches of her throat again. "Stop asking inane questions."

"But I have to ask something. I don't have a clue what's going on here. Please, tell me what you want."

"All will become obvious in a little while. Now, take several steps backwards."

Reluctantly, Paula did as she was ordered and soon found the ledge of the building resting against the back of her calves. She glanced sideways at the drop below her, and another lump swiftly settled into her throat. "What now? What do you want?"

He removed something else from the inside of his jacket. It was a reporter's notebook and a pen. He thrust the items towards her and ordered, "Write this down."

Her hand trembled violently as she took the notebook and pen.

"I hate my life as it is, I can't take any more of this. I loathe my husband and need to get away from my suffocating marriage. Don't mourn my loss, I'll be in a far better place where I'm going."

She started to write the words only to stop several times. The knife digging into her throat forced her to continue. "Why? I can't write this. No one will believe I took the coward's way out. No one, you hear me?"

"I hear you, and you're wrong. Do you know the statistics of students committing suicide every year? It runs into thousands."

"Those people don't have a loving husband at home who they can turn to, not like me."

The man laughed. "Don't bullshit me, Paula."

Her eyes narrowed when her name left his lips. "I know you, don't I?"

He nodded. "You do. Don't worry, I'll make this as painless as possible. If, however, you decide to put up a struggle, there's no telling how this might end."

"I can't. No, I refuse to go to my death like this. It's not my time to leave this earth yet, you can't force me to do it."

"Can't I? Are you sure about that?" He took another step towards her.

The knife nicked her throat, and she felt the trickle of blood ooze down her neck.

She retreated as far back as she could, but the wall prevented any further movement. She feared her life was about to end if she didn't put up a fight, but how could she? One move and he'd probably slice her throat open, or would he? Why make her write a suicide note if his intention was to kill her? She lashed out with her arm, caught him in the chest, but the knife didn't waver, and it nicked her throat a second time.

"Stop, don't do this to me. Why are you doing it? Why? What have I ever done to you?"

"Plenty, none of them good."

"Let me make amends, correct things. I don't want to die."

"I've got news for you, no one wants to die, but it comes to us all in the end."

"Are you sure? There must be a way around this, there has to be. I'll do anything to get out of this, anything."

There was a pause. Had she got him thinking? Was there a light at the end of the tunnel for her to reach for?

After a few moments' pause, he shook his head. "No, it's far too late to alter the course of things now."

"What course? What are you talking about?"

"Shut up. The more you try to bend my ear, the worse it will become."

"Are you for real? How can things possibly get any worse than they are right now? How?" Her voice hit another level as the fear escalated. She sensed things were getting out of control fast.

The knife waved before her eyes. She blinked several times and then decided to keep her eyes wide open, to view things as they happened. If she was going out this way she wanted to see how and who to come back to haunt. Her hand shot out and hooked onto the balaclava. The man stepped back, but she held firmly and yanked the woollen piece of material from his head.

She gasped. "You. How could you do this? Stop it now, you've had your fun. It's time to put an end to this."

He laughed. Fury raging in his eyes at being discovered,

or so she presumed. Taking two steps towards her, he shoved her.

Tumbling… she fell backwards, and the world plummeted around her before she hit the ground, then there was nothing…

CHAPTER 1

"Closing this last case has caused me a right headache. I've got Roberts jumping up and down, expecting the files on his desk ASAP. I don't know whether I'm coming or going today," Katy complained.

Charlie sat opposite her in her office and shook her head. "I'm always telling you that you should delegate more. Look at you, you're stressed to the hilt, and here's me, sitting here, all nice and calm."

Katy cradled her chin between her thumb and forefinger. "Are you giving me the green light to send more work your way, Charlie?"

"Why not? I would if I were your senior officer. You have my permission to use me and abuse me."

Katy raised an eyebrow and pushed back her chair. "I didn't want to push you too hard too soon. You've not long passed your sergeant's exam and…"

Charlie raised a hand to cut her off. "May I remind you that was a few months ago now. Stop trying to keep me wrapped up in cotton wool. I think Mum would be disappointed in you if she thought you didn't have the confidence in my ability."

Katy's mouth dropped open for a moment or two. Snapping it shut again, she blurted out, "That's bollocks, and you know it. I have every faith in you. Maybe in the beginning I was a tad guilty of 'protecting you' but not recently."

Cocking an eyebrow as if in disbelief, Charlie sighed. "Who are you trying to kid?"

Katy wagged a finger from side to side. "All right, laying my cards on the table, I have been a little conscious of not heaping pressure on your shoulders with the last case, only because of what you're going through at home. Some inspectors might think their partner's personal life has no right to interfere with their work... not me."

"In all fairness, I don't recall a time when my personal life has ever affected the way I function around here. If anything, my past speaks for itself."

Katy winced at the reference to the degrading experience Charlie had been through at the hands of her mother's greatest nemesis, the evil Unicorn. "Sorry, this has nothing to do with that, and you know it."

"Do I? I'm over it, I've been over it for years now. Between you and my mother... well, you appear to be the ones who have the issue regarding that stage of my life, not me."

"That's unfair."

"Is it? I stopped having nightmares about what that bastard did to me a long time ago. If anyone still has an issue with what happened nearly ten years ago now, it's you and Mum."

"I'm sorry you feel that way, Charlie. In my defence, that's not what this is about, it has to do with you breaking up with Brandon and..."

Charlie raised her hand again. "We're simply going

around in circles, Katy, I'm over him. Yes, he's still around, calling at the house now and again to pick up the odd bits and pieces that he left behind in his rush to run back home to Mummy and Daddy, but I can cope with it. Stop mollycoddling me, I get enough of that when I speak to Mum every weekend. Anyway, I wasn't going to tell you this…"

Katy frowned and prompted her to continue, "Tell me what? No… you're not thinking of jacking it all in and leaving the team, are you?"

Charlie heaved out a large breath that puffed out her cheeks. "Jesus, will you give it a rest, please? I'm devoted to this team, as much as you are. What I was about to say before you rudely interrupted me was that…" Charlie hesitated, prolonging Katy's agony even longer.

"What? Come on."

"I wanted to tell you that I'm seeing someone else."

Katy sprang forward in her chair. "What? Well, that didn't take you long to get over your broken heart, did it?" Her mobile rang. She examined the caller ID and groaned.

Charlie swiftly leapt out of her chair and headed for the door. "Saved by the bell. I'll leave you to it. Do you want me to switch everything off?"

"If this is what I think it is, I'm betting we'll be called into action soon."

Charlie glanced at her watch and groaned. "It's past seven-thirty."

"Do you have a date this evening?"

"No, I was merely stating a fact."

The phone rang for the fourth time. "I've got to get this, otherwise Patti is going to be livid with me."

Charlie gave her the thumbs-up and left the room, closing the door behind her.

"Sorry, Patti, I was on the other line," Katy said.

15

"You've always got some excuse for not taking my calls lately, Katy, you're giving me a complex."

Katy laughed. "That's your fault, not mine, for being so sensitive. What's up? Before you tell me, I need to tell you that I was just about to head home for the evening."

"You were? Going anywhere nice, were you?"

"I said home. Why?"

"I have an interesting crime scene I'd like you to take a look at, but if you haven't got the time, I'll find someone else."

"Good luck with that one, we're short-staffed and up shit creek. Interesting how?"

"You'll find out when you get here."

"Where's here?"

"At the university just up the road from the hospital. Jackson's University."

"I know it. I'm also aware that I'm not going to get anything further from you over the phone. Charlie and I will be with you in fifteen minutes at the most."

"Glad to hear it. My guys are in the process of putting up the marquees now. See you soon."

Katy was left holding the phone, listening to a dead line. She heaved out a weary sigh and slipped on her jacket. After tidying up the papers on her desk and shoving them in her to-do tray, she left the office and went in search of her partner. "Are you good to go?"

"Where to?"

"Jackson's University. Don't ask, that's as much as I know."

"Do we have a choice? I mean, we've already done a ten-hour shift today. My brain was beginning to shut down, now I have to wind it up again."

"I hear what you're saying. Push through the pain, and

we'll go over there, have a quick shufti, and then call it a night, okay?"

"Why don't I believe you?"

THEY ARRIVED, under the assistance of their siren, with five minutes to spare. After throwing on their protective gear, they were escorted to the crime scene beyond the cordon by a uniformed officer.

"Ah, nice of you to join me here, ladies. Sorry to intrude on your plans for the evening," Patti said. She was standing at the doorway of the marquee, issuing instructions to a couple of members of her team.

The two male techs departed, and Katy and Charlie followed Patti into the tent.

"What have we got here?" Katy asked.

"A dead female, who at first glance decided to jump off the roof of the building," Patti informed them. She took a step closer to the twisted body of the young woman and crouched close to her head.

Katy and Charlie followed suit on the other side of the corpse.

"At first glance?" Katy asked.

"That's what I said. Look at the marks on her neck, there's blood there. In my opinion, there is no reason for it being there."

"What if she caught her neck on the edge as she fell? Or if she fell against the building and tried to reach out and scratched her neck in the process? Would you have the full use of your limbs during a dramatic fall like that?"

"I believe you would, yes, within reason. And no, I don't think the wounds are self-inflicted. Of course, at this early stage, I might be talking out of my arse."

Katy's brow furrowed into a deep frown as she forced her

brain to notch up into another gear. "Are they knife wounds? Are you telling me someone held a knife to her throat... forcing her to jump? To take her own life?"

Patti stood and shrugged. "That would be my initial deduction, although not my official one. You know me, I like to tie everything up into a nice bow and not throw inept assumptions around at this stage of the game."

"That'll be the day, you throwing anything inept around, be it assumptions or otherwise, for that matter."

Patti smiled and took a bow. "Why thank you, Katy, I'll take that as a huge compliment, knowing that you hand them out as rarely as hen's teeth."

"What the fu...?"

Patti grinned. "Just teasing, there's no need for you to get all uppity with me."

"I have no intention of getting uppity with you. So, is this why you chose to call us out so late in our working day? You believe this is a suspicious death?" Katy surveyed the woman's body and noticed something in her hand. "Hang on, what's that?"

Patti crouched again and eased the woman's hand open, but not before she had called on one of the techs to photograph the hand first. "Interesting."

"What is?" Katy asked impatiently.

"It's a suicide note."

"A what? What does it say?"

I HATE my life as it is, I can't take any more of this. I loathe my husband and need to get away from my suffocating marriage.

Don't mourn my loss, I'll be in a far better place where I'm going.

· · ·

"REALLY?" Katy was at a loss what to say or think next. All three of them remained silent for a few minutes until Katy said, "So what are we saying here, that she tried to slit her throat and when that failed, she wrote a suicide note and threw herself over the edge?" Something wasn't sitting right with her once she'd voiced the potential scenario. "Would the note still be in her hand after falling that far?"

Patti stared at her and shrugged again. "All we can do is work with the evidence we have in front of us."

"Okay, I can see why you called us now. Who found her?"

"A lecturer on his way to his car."

"Is he still around?" Katy tried to recall seeing anyone close to the cordon. She couldn't. Yes, there was a crowd further back, but they would have been the usual rubber-neckers who always seemed to pop up at scenes of this nature.

"Last I saw, the uniformed officer was putting him in the back of his car."

"Do you need us here any more?"

"No. Let me know what he says before you shoot off, if you would?" Patti replied.

Katy nodded and left the tent with Charlie. "How are you for time?"

Charlie batted away her question with a limp wrist. "I'm fine. You worry too much. I'm not going anywhere. This is intriguing, isn't it?"

"It is. I just hope the intrigue doesn't ultimately turn to frustration."

Charlie laughed. "I think you're guilty of tempting fate there."

"I hope not. Okay, let's see what the prof has to say."

They disrobed and threw their suits, shoe covers and gloves into the waiting black sack close to the cordon.

"There should be a witness around here, in the back of a patrol car, I believe," Katy said.

"Yes, ma'am. Over to the right. Gentleman's name is Donald Tremor."

"Great, thanks."

They walked across the gravelled area to the car. Before Katy opened the back door to speak to the witness, she turned to survey the area behind her. Her gaze drifted up to the roof of the building closest to where the body had landed.

"What would you say that is? Eighty to a hundred feet or more?"

"Closer to a hundred, I would say, not that I'm an expert on heights, they scare the shit out of me," Charlie lowered her voice to reply.

"After that maniac holding a gun to my head at the top of a building, I can't say I'm enamoured with them either."

"Sorry, I'd forgotten all about that incident. You were brave, and dare I say it, my heroine that day."

Katy wrinkled her nose and smiled. "Gee, thanks." She opened the back door and bent down to speak to the gentleman in the rear seat. "Mr Tremor, is it?"

"Yes, Donald. Are you the officer in charge?"

"That's right. I'm DI Katy Foster, and this is my partner, DS Charlie Simpkins. Are you up to having a chat with us?"

"Of course. Such a dreadful event to stumble across at that time of day." He hopped out of the car and stretched his legs, one at a time, then raised his arms above his head and doubled over to drop to his ankles. He straightened up again and issued an apology, "Sorry, I get tight and full of tension if I sit down for long. My physio said every time it happens, I need to stretch out, get my limbs working more like normal. Use it or lose it as the saying goes."

"Understandable. Sorry to have kept you so long. Can you tell us what happened?"

"I finished my lectures at around five, stayed behind in the class marking some work, and left the university at around six-thirty. I never expected to walk around the corner and see her lying there, in the dark."

"Did you see anyone else hanging around?"

"No, the coast was clear. I was terrified one of the other pupils might come around the corner and see her. Fortunately, that never happened. I rang nine-nine-nine right away and was relieved when a patrol showed up within minutes. That's when it hit me. I was a mess when they asked me what had gone on, I couldn't tell them. All I knew was that I found her lying there. Did she jump?"

"We're not sure at present. The pathologist is still assessing the scene. Did you know her?"

"Yes, she was one of my students. One of the older students in my lectures."

Charlie whipped out her notebook, and Katy asked the obvious question, "You can give us her name then?"

"Oh yes, sorry, maybe I should have told you that from the outset rather than calling her 'her' all the time. She's Paula Lowe. This is her first year back at university. She used to be a secretary but was keen to improve herself. I can't imagine her taking her own life like this. I think that's why I'm struggling here."

"You know her well enough to know what type of character she was?"

"She was fun, outgoing, always had a good word to say about her fellow students. Always assisting them either before or after class, sharing her worldly experience with them, if you like. God, I can't believe she's dead."

"Would she have come to you if she was distressed or in any kind of trouble?"

"I'd like to think so. You get a feel for when a student isn't coping with their coursework. I never got that impression with her in the slightest. She was one of the top five students in my lectures. The first to raise a question if something didn't sit right with her. Loved to challenge the coursework which, believe it or not, is music to a lecturer's ears if appropriately actioned. I would go so far as to say she was in line to pass her course with flying colours, in the top five percent, and yet, she felt the need to take her own life without reaching out and seeking help."

"We're keeping an open mind on that at the moment, sir. Were you aware that she was married?"

"Of course. I've met Adrian a few times, he seems a decent enough chap. Supported her coming back to university. Not many husbands would do the same."

"So there were no problems between them then?"

He sighed, and his mouth turned down at the sides. "You think there might have been? I can only go by what I saw. She never mentioned there were any issues in her marriage. Would he have willingly visited the uni if he was dead set against her attending the lectures or enrolling in the course?"

"Possibly not. At the moment, we're scrabbling around for possible leads. I don't suppose you happen to know where she lives, do you?"

"I thought you might ask. I checked out her personnel file and wrote down her address for you."

"That's super-efficient, I appreciate it."

He handed Katy the slip of paper with the address written on it and put his hand back in his jacket pocket.

Katy decided to leave it there. The man looked shell-shocked and chilled to the bone. "If you give my partner your address, we'll get a uniformed officer to call round to see you in the next forty-eight hours to take down a statement, if that's all right with you?"

"I was about to ask you if you'd like me to supply you with further details. Can I go now? It's my wife's birthday, and we've got friends arriving at nine for dinner. She'll be going nuts, stressing out that I'm not there to help out."

"Of course. Sorry to hold you up for so long. I hope this doesn't spoil your evening too much."

"It will, but I'll put on a front rather than suffer the wrath of Eliza Tremor."

Katy smiled. "Take care, sir. Are you all right to drive home or would you rather hitch a ride with a patrol?"

"No, please don't concern yourself, you have enough on your plate as it is without running around after me. My car is only over there. I'm a lot calmer now than I was half an hour ago, so I should be fine to drive home."

"If you're sure? Thanks for hanging around to speak with us, especially as you have dinner plans for this evening."

"It's not a problem. Happy to oblige, well, you know what I mean, in the circumstances."

"I do. Drive carefully, and thanks again for your time this evening."

Katy and Charlie watched the professor walk away, his shoulders slouched and his head bowed.

"It's hit him hard," Charlie said.

"It has. Are you sure you're okay for time?"

"We're out here now, let's do what we have to do to get the investigation started. Stop worrying about my social life, or lack of it. What about AJ, should you ring him?"

"Yeah, I was thinking the same. I'll do it from the car. I hope he doesn't throw a wobbly, this is the second time I've been late home this week."

"Problems at home?"

They walked back to the car and jumped in.

"Not really. I try to stick to a routine, more for Georgie's sake than mine. She has a check-up with the heart specialist next week. I've booked the day off, I hope that's okay?"

Charlie laughed. "You're asking for my permission? Are you nuts? You do what you have to do to keep your family happy and healthy, Katy, that's the main criteria, right?"

"If you say so. Okay, let's see what the husband has to say about what's happened here this evening. We need to go in there with an open mind on this one."

"What about the suicide note, are you going to mention that to him?"

Katy started the engine and pulled onto the main road. "I'll see how it goes. I'm glad Patti called me, it's definitely going to be an intriguing case for us to sink our teeth into. That reminds me," she turned the car around and parked again. "I promised to fill Patti in, she'll have a fit if I don't keep to my word. I won't be long."

KATY DREW up outside a semi-detached house in a quiet road not too far from the university. The house was lit up, upstairs and down. To the front of the property was a small garden that was covered in slate chippings and a few plant pots dotted around the area.

"Low maintenance, a sign that busy people live here," Katy said. She winked at Charlie who shook her head.

"There are no flies on you, boss."

Katy grinned and then her serious face emerged as she rang the bell. A man in his mid-twenties sporting a stubbled chin and cropped brown hair opened it a few seconds later.

"Can I help?"

"Mr Lowe?" Katy enquired.

"That's right, and you are?"

Katy and Charlie produced their warrant cards.

"DI Katy Foster and DS Charlie Simpkins. Would it be all right if we come in and speak to you for a moment, sir?"

"About what?" He glanced over Katy's shoulder at the car and the road beyond. "Oh God, this isn't about Paula, is it?"

Katy nodded. "It really would be better if we spoke inside, Mr Lowe."

"It's Adrian. Okay, you'd better come in. Jesus, I can sense what's coming next. It's never a good sign when coppers show up mob-handed at your door. Sorry, that came out the wrong way."

"Don't worry, we're not easily offended."

Katy and Charlie followed him into the lounge.

He threw himself onto the end cushion of the giant corner sofa and invited them to take a seat at the other end. "Is Paula all right?"

Katy inhaled a steadying breath and let it seep out slowly. "I'm sorry to have to be the bearer of bad news, but this evening, your wife lost her life in what would appear to be a tragic accident."

He stared at her for what seemed a lifetime, all the while shaking his head. Tears surfaced and brimmed, threatening to fall. Eventually, he opened his mouth and whispered, "No, this can't be right. She can't be dead. She just can't be."

"I'm sorry, there's no doubting her identity, one of her lecturers identified her at the scene."

"Which one?"

"Professor Tremor, do you know him?"

"Yes, we've met once or twice. Was he there when it happened?" He gasped, and his lip curled up. "Don't tell me they were having an affair?"

"Ah, no, I think you've got the wrong end of the stick. He found her, she was lying in the road, close to where he had parked his car."

"Lying in the road? Did someone knock her down? Why

25

can't you just come right out and tell me all the facts, instead of stringing it out, prolonging my agony?"

"I apologise, that truly wasn't my intention. The facts as we know them at this stage of the investigation are that Paula was found in the road. All the indications are that your wife committed suicide."

He bounced forward and teetered on the edge of the sofa, his elbows digging into his thighs. "What? No, you're wrong, she would never do that. She had too much to live for. Why would you even consider it?"

"Because we found a suicide note in her hand."

He shook his head over and over and stared at Katy. "I can't believe what you're saying. I spoke to her this evening, she didn't sound any different to me. Surely, I would have picked up on something during the call. I didn't. She was just Paula."

"Did you have a happy marriage?"

"What type of question is that? Of course we did. I was supporting her while she went back to uni. If I wasn't happy about it, I would have put my foot down."

Katy sat there, studying his reactions, judging whether he held eye contact with her or not. She decided to be brutally honest with him. "As I said, a suicide note was found in her hand."

"Are you going to tell me what it said?"

"It says that she'd had enough and that she loathed you. She also mentioned that she found her marriage to be suffocating her."

"What utter bollocks. There's no way she would write, let alone think, that."

"Okay. We're going to have to take your word for that. You mentioned that you spoke with her this evening. Can you tell me how the conversation went?"

His forearms rested on his thighs, and he clenched his

hands together until the knuckles turned white. After a substantial pause, he finally expelled a long sigh. "It wasn't good. I expected her home earlier, and she said she had stayed behind to speak to a lecturer. Shit, I ended the call in a foul mood, and now… I will never lay eyes on her again to apologise. Wait, she sent me a text a few minutes after the call had ended." He left his seat and collected his phone from the large rectangular oak coffee table a few feet in front of him. "Here it is. She told me she was fed up with being treated like a dog and that she had her own life to lead. She'd be home when she wanted to come home."

"Did you respond to the message?"

"No. I was seething. I've answered back before in anger and regretted my decision. I thought I would have it out with her when she finally came home. Now that's never going to happen, and I feel like shit. I have a knot so tight in my stomach, as though my intestines are twisted over and over. Jesus, how could the evening end like this?"

"Can I see the message?"

"I have nothing to hide. Here." He handed Katy the phone, his hand trembling as he gave it to her.

She read the message herself, and it was easy to detect the tone behind what she was reading. "I'm sorry this will be the last message you will have received from her." Katy paused to search for what to say next. The last thing she wanted to do was upset the man more than he was already. "I have to ask if your wife had mentioned if she was having problems with anyone lately."

His brow furrowed. "I don't understand. Why would you want to know that? Do you believe she was having an affair behind my back? No, that wouldn't make sense, not unless the other person was married and the wife found out and killed her in a rage. Sorry, my mind is playing tricks on me, thinking up all sorts of scenarios and explanations as to why she is no longer with us. Was she? Having an affair?"

Katy held her hands up in front of her. "As I said, we're at the start of our investigation. All we have to go on so far is what you've told us this evening."

"Let me tell you this, we loved each other, despite what that message bloody says. I don't know where that has come from. Yes, we had a slight argument this evening, but most couples let rip now and again. It doesn't mean they suddenly hate one another, does it? We're all entitled to blow a fuse, only to make up later, aren't we?"

"I suppose so. When you received the message and rang her this evening, where were you?"

He pointed at the floor and said adamantly, "Here. Oh, I get it, what's wrong? Now you think I bloody killed her and staged her suicide, is that it?"

Katy was astonished by the vehemency in his words and the speed at which he'd come up with the idea for consideration. "No. All I'm trying to ascertain is how your wife came to end her life, if that is indeed the case."

"What evidence do you have to the contrary? There must be something, otherwise you wouldn't be asking such questions and, yes, my father used to be in the Force, and we've had many a chat over the years about the type of questions he's had to ask people in order to get the truth out of them."

"Ah, I see. Who is your father?"

"Frank Lowe. He used to be a detective in the Met."

Katy nodded. She recognised the name but struggled to recall the face. "I think I remember him. Did he retire early?"

"Yes, he got caught up in a gang war in the city and was shot several times. Thankfully, his partner got him to hospital before he lost too much blood. The docs were able to remove the bullets within half an hour of him arriving there, but he was forced to retire early as one of the bullets nicked his femur, just missed the artery, it did. He was lucky it wasn't a centimetre higher, that's what the doctor told him. Anyway, they gave him the option of retiring early, and he jumped at the chance. Between you and me, though, he's always regretted that decision as funds are often tight for him and Mum. She had to go out and find a little job herself, just to make ends meet."

"Sorry to hear that. The public are always under the impression that a copper's pension is massive. It isn't, it all depends on how many years you've contributed to it."

"That's right. Dad was a late starter. He admits he was an idiot when he was younger, thought his pension would look after itself as a lot of people do, but the harsh reality soon set in. Now, with the bills rocketing, they're even considering selling up the family home, the house where I was brought up. Mind you, it's old and needs a lot of repairs. So they might as well get shot of it and downsize, if they can sell the old place. That's not going to be easy in the current climate either."

"I'm sure things will work out for them in the end. Send him my best regards when you see him."

"I will. I'm hoping that now you've heard who my father is you'll cut me some slack."

Katy smiled. "It was never my intention to point the finger at you. With your knowledge of how the Force works, I'm sure you'll appreciate our need to dig deep this early into the investigation."

"I do. But please, do your digging elsewhere, I'm above board, I promise. Anyway, you can't leave things there, something must have caused you to have doubts about my wife's death. Are you going to tell me what that is?"

Katy glanced at Charlie who was busy taking notes. Her partner sensed her looking and gave her an encouraging nod.

Katy turned her attention back to Adrian. "I wouldn't

normally divulge this information this early during a case, but when we showed up at the crime scene tonight, the pathologist found some unusual marks on your wife's neck."

"Marks? Such as?"

"She wasn't willing to commit to that just yet," Katy replied, purposefully holding back the truth until Patti had performed the post-mortem.

"You can't leave it there. What sort of marks? Scratches? Gouges? You have to tell me now, otherwise it's going to play on my mind after you leave."

"Small nicks. That's all I'm willing to share with you at this time. Are you up for answering some more questions?"

"If I must. Let's get this over with. What do you want to know?"

"Was she close to anyone at uni?"

"A few of them used to hang out together during the breaks and after their lectures. Don't ask me who they were, though, I don't have a clue. No doubt her friend list will be in her phone, do you have that? Or wasn't it with her when she was found?"

"I think it was there, we'll get onto Forensics about that, see what they can give us. What about friends outside of uni?"

"There's only really one, that's Dawn. Yes, I have her number in my phone as we used to go out in a foursome with her and her fella, Simon." He picked up the mobile that Katy had returned to the table and scrolled through his contact list. "Here you go."

Katy took the phone again and tilted it so that Charlie could jot down the relevant information. "Thanks, we'll get in touch with her, see if she can tell us anything."

"Ah, I get you, friends sharing secrets, keen to keep things from their partners, that kind of stuff."

"Exactly. What about Paula's parents, are they still alive?"

"Shit! I forgot all about them, they'll need to be told, won't they? How the effing hell am I supposed to do that? Tell them that their only child is now dead? Their cherished daughter, she meant the world to them, especially her father. He's a bank manager. He was a high-flier in the city at one stage before he took up his new post about five years ago."

"Do you want to tell them or would you rather we do it for you?"

"Would you mind? I bloody wouldn't know where to start. I can't believe I'm taking this so well, it hasn't really hit me yet. My mate was the same when he lost his mum to breast cancer last year. He went about his normal day for a few weeks, then one day at work, he collapsed in a heap. I ended up on the floor with him, rocking him back and forth like a baby while he sobbed."

"It will probably hit you once we leave. Can we call anyone to be with you? Another family member? What about your father? I would imagine he'd be a huge help, given the opportunity."

"No, I'd rather not. I need to get used to the news myself first. I know that probably sounds weird."

Katy offered up a weak smile. "It doesn't, not in the slightest. Another question if I may. I don't suppose Paula ever mentioned feeling scared of anyone at uni, did she?"

"Scared? As if someone was about to attack her?"

"Yes, was there anyone creeping her out, stalking her, maybe? Trying to get close to her?"

"If there was, she hid the fact from me. I would tell you if anything came to mind."

"Okay, we're going to leave it there now. I'll give you one of my cards, get in touch if you need to discuss the case further or think you can add anything that we failed to cover here tonight."

The three of them rose from their seats and walked into the hallway.

Adrian held the front door open for them and let out another sigh. "Thank you for coming to see me in person. It's good to know that you'll be in charge of the investigation, Inspector. Please, don't let our family down. If Paula didn't commit suicide, which I doubt she did, then please find the person responsible for taking her from us."

"We'll do our very best. Reach out if you need me, day or night, okay?"

"Thank you. I'll do that."

They left the house and returned to the car.

Once inside, Charlie asked, "Do you believe him?"

Katy swallowed and nodded. She glanced back at the house and said, "I think so, yes. There's only one way of seeing if he's telling us the truth or not and that's to speak with the parents, plus her best friend."

"I have a gut feeling her best friend is going to hold the key on this one. Saying that, I've been known to get things wrong in the past."

Katy tapped her thigh. "Not that often, and stop putting yourself down. Are you up for making another call this evening? It would bug me going home now without telling her parents."

"I think you're right. Let's do it."

Katy noticed the clock on the dash as she turned the steering wheel ninety degrees and pulled away from the kerb; it was already eight-thirty. "Shit! Doesn't time fly when you're having fun?"

Charlie chuckled. "I hadn't noticed the having fun part, but who am I to doubt your word?"

"As I keep telling you, you're a very wise young lady."

CHAPTER 2

Katy knocked on the front door of the detached house on the exclusive estate. "Nice place, must have cost a bob or two."

"I was thinking the same. I think Brandon's uncle lives around here somewhere, he runs his own accountancy firm."

The door opened, and a woman in her sixties frowned at them. She closed the door to a bit so only her head was showing through the gap. The gesture was delayed as though she'd only just realised what the time was and there were two strangers standing on her doorstep.

Katy produced her warrant card. "Hello, Mrs Falkirk. I'm DI Katy Foster, and this is my partner, DS Charlie Simpkins. Would it be possible for us to come in and speak with you, please?"

"Oh… is there anything wrong? I mean, it's not every day the police show up at my door."

"It would be better if we spoke inside. Is your husband at home?"

"Yes, has he done something wrong? Is that why you're here?"

Katy sighed inwardly, as if this task wasn't hard enough. "Please, Mrs Falkirk, inside would be preferable."

She leaned her head back and bellowed for her husband to join them.

"What's wrong, Denise? I was busy in my study."

"Sorry to disturb you, Mr Falkirk," Katy jumped in before his wife had the chance to speak. "I'm DI Katy Foster from the Met Police. Would it be possible to speak to you both inside?"

"Of course. Denise, what are you thinking? Let them in, for God's sake. What's the matter with you, woman?"

"I... umm... I just have a feeling this is going to be bad news."

"Well, we won't know until they've told us, will we? Now step back and let the ladies in."

Mrs Falkirk reluctantly moved into the spacious tiled hallway, and her husband showed them into a vast lounge-cum-dining room at the rear of the property that was tastefully decorated in rich burgundy and gold. There was a fire ablaze in the woodburning stove close to the seating area.

"Please, won't you take a seat and tell us what this is all about? Does it have anything to do with my work?"

Katy smiled and shook her head. She waited until everyone had sat and then said, "I'm sorry to have to inform you that your daughter, Paula, lost her life this evening."

Mrs Falkirk gasped and clutched her husband's hand.

He stared at Katy and shook his head, the disbelief and grief evident in his lined features. "No," he whispered, his voice sounding very distant.

"I'm sorry."

"How?" Mrs Falkirk asked between sobs.

"We were called to the university earlier. Her body was found at the bottom of a building. We're treating it as a possible suicide until the post-mortem has been performed."

"Never in a million years," Mr Falkirk shouted, incensed.

His wife clutched his hand tighter, until her knuckles changed colour. "Not our Paula. I agree, she wouldn't. She was one of the happiest people I know, nothing ever fazed her. There must be some kind of mistake. There must be."

Mrs Falkirk broke down again, and her husband released a hand from her grasp, threw an arm around her shoulders and pulled her tightly.

"I agree wholeheartedly with what my wife has said. There must be some kind of mistake. Why do you think it was sui… suicide?"

"We found a suicide note in her hand and put two and two together with the fact that she likely jumped from the roof of the building." Katy tried her hardest to sound convincing, but all the time her stomach was doing somersaults, knowing that they could indeed be dealing with a murder inquiry and not a suspected suicide as first thought, if only fleetingly, at the scene.

"I find this utterly incredulous. I demand to see that note," Mr Falkirk said.

Katy removed her phone from her pocket and showed him the note via the photo she had taken at the university earlier.

He adamantly shook his head. "That's not her handwriting. Or maybe it is, the writing is kind of shaky. What do you think, love?"

Mrs Falkirk sniffled and stared up at her husband, her eyes all puffy and swollen. "I can't tell. If it's not, what does this mean, Lesley?"

"If she didn't write it, surely it means that someone killed her and placed that note with her in the hope that the police would believe that she had committed suicide. There's no way our baby would do such a dreadful thing. Umm… has Adrian, her husband, been informed?"

"Yes, he's the one who gave us your address."

"And what did he say?"

"He doesn't believe she would have committed suicide either."

"If we're all agreed, then you need to start taking us seriously."

"How close were you to Paula?" Katy raised a hand. "By that I mean, did she confide in you?"

"Of course she did. As a family we're, sorry, we *were* very close," Mrs Falkirk said, correcting her tense.

"Did she mention lately if there was anything troubling her?" Katy asked.

"What? Enough for her to want to kill herself, is that what you're asking?" Mr Falkirk blasted.

"What I'm asking is, if she had any problems, such as was she concerned about anyone she knew who was pestering her, anything like that?"

The couple fell silent as they thought and looked at each other.

"I can't think of anything, can you, love?" Mr Falkirk asked his wife.

"No, I'm sure she would have told us. She was a good student, devoted to her studies, determined to improve her chances of getting a better job. What did Adrian say about all of this? Did you ask him the same question?" Mrs Falkirk asked.

"I did. He couldn't think of anyone. He was as shocked about her death as you are but couldn't give us any leads to go on."

"Are you talking about a possible stalker perhaps?" Mrs Falkirk asked.

"Possibly, at this early stage it's impossible to tell what has occurred. If there is anything pricking your mind about a recent conversation you had with your daughter that caused you to have any concerns, it would be good to know."

After several seconds' pause, the couple shook their heads.

"I can't think of anything, can you, Den?"

Mrs Falkirk tearfully glanced up at her husband, appearing to be dazed and confused. "No, not at this moment in time. I can't believe she's gone. Why Paula? She's never harmed anyone, spoken ill of anyone, nothing along those lines at all. I can't believe someone… would take her life."

She broke down again, and her husband pulled her head against his chest and soothed her greying hair with his hand. He stared at the floor in front of him, shellshocked.

"I can't believe it either. That our daughter is no longer with us. It's terrible to imagine that we will never hug or kiss her again," Mr Falkirk said. He gulped and shook his head over and over, obviously trying to hold back his own emotions while he put his wife's grief first. "Where do we go from here?"

"We'll begin the investigation in earnest, question the dean in the morning, it's getting late now."

"Won't that be too late? What if the killer is still out there? Couldn't they strike again? Take someone else's daughter?"

"That's always a possibility. If we call in the morning, we can view any footage available on campus via the cameras. Hopefully that will give us a lead or two to go on."

"In other words, there's very little else you can do, or are willing to do, given the time?"

"Yes. Don't worry, my team and I will hit the ground running in the morning, first thing."

"Glad to hear it. It still doesn't sit well with me that the killer is out there, running loose still."

Katy smiled tautly. "Is there anything else you can tell us about your daughter that might help the investigation?"

Mr Falkirk inclined his head and frowned. "Such as?"

"Perhaps you can tell us what her marriage was like?" Katy asked tentatively.

"What? Are you saying that he's under the microscope now?" Mrs Falkirk shot back.

"No. It's important for us to cover every angle right out of the starting gate. If there were problems in her marriage, then we should know about them."

The Falkirks shook their heads in unison.

"They had the odd spat, like every couple does," Mr Falkirk admitted. "But Adrian is a good lad, we were exceedingly happy with the choice our daughter made selecting him as a husband. He treated her well, on the whole."

"I have to ask, had either of them been unfaithful in the past?"

"Definitely not," Mr Falkirk said, his voice rising. "They loved one another and would never have done the dirty on each other."

"Thank you. Okay, I think we've covered everything now. Are you going to be all right?"

"We'll never be all right again, not after hearing this news. No one wants to outlive their own child, Inspector," Mr Falkirk added.

"I know. Again, you have our condolences, but I also want to give you the assurance that we will do our very best to find the person responsible."

"And soon, I hope."

"Yes. We'll leave you now. Thank you for seeing us at such short notice."

"Please, please, don't let our daughter's death go unsolved. You hear of so many cases these days that have no resolution to them. I don't want our daughter's life to have been lost in vain."

"I assure you, we're going to ensure that doesn't happen."

Katy and Charlie rose from their seats, and Mr Falkirk showed them to the front door.

"I agree with my wife, please do all you can to solve this case and give us the closure we need to get on with our lives. Our daughter meant the world to us, of course she did, every parent will surely say the same, but I really mean it, she was our everything. We were so proud of her taking the decision to go back to university at her age. Her head wasn't in the right place to attend further education directly after leaving school. She took a year off to travel the world, before returning and settling down with Adrian. He's a good man, don't think badly of him, he's not capable of harming our daughter, of that much I'm certain."

"Thank you for the reassurance. Take care of each other, Mr Falkirk."

"Don't worry about us, my wife will be fine, I'll make sure of that."

"Here's my card, ring me if you need to chat at all or if you think of anything else we should know that may help our investigation."

"We'll be in touch, don't worry."

Katy and Charlie left the house.

Katy let out a huge sigh on the way back to the car. "I wasn't at my best in there, was I?"

Charlie smiled over the top of the car. "It's been a long day. You did fine, stop doubting yourself. I take it we're going to call it a day now?"

"I have to say yes, even though I'd much rather plough on and speak to Paula's best friend. We'll do that in the morning and go to the university as well. It's almost ten, and I'm dead on my feet."

"I'm not too bad. I could go and see the best friend tonight, on the way home, if you wanted me to?"

"Are you sure you wouldn't mind?"

"Not at all."

"I'll drop you back to the station and head home then, if you're one hundred percent sure?"

"I am. Stop worrying about me, I wouldn't have suggested it if I felt too bad. You go home to your family and get some rest."

"You're a star, Charlie, where would I be without you by my side?"

"Lost most of the time. It's fine, you worry too much."

KATY GAVE Charlie instructions on what to ask the best friend and dropped her partner off at the station. A twinge of guilt settled in her stomach all the way home. She asked Charlie to give her a call after her visit was over. Katy relaxed during the journey with a love song compilation playing on the stereo. She was looking forward to cuddling up with AJ for half an hour before she went to bed. Not feeling very hungry, she'd probably give dinner a miss when she got in.

There was a strange car sitting in her usual parking space outside the house which ticked her off. Some heavy breathing later, she finally found another space a few doors up and walked back to her home. She let herself in and paused when she opened the inner door to the hallway. A woman's laughter filtered through the house from the kitchen. Katy removed her shoes and coat, tucked them away and walked into the kitchen to see what was going on.

"Oh, hi," she said, taking in the young blonde sitting opposite AJ.

He left his chair and came over to give her a kiss. "Hi, you didn't ring. I was expecting your call."

"Sorry, I was too tired, I just wanted to get home quickly, without delay. Am I interrupting something?" She noted the fact that AJ had obviously invited this young woman to eat dinner with him.

"No, sorry. I should introduce you. This is my new assistant, Lily Bradshaw. You remember me telling you that I'd offered her the job, don't you?"

"I think so," Katy replied, doubting her ability to think straight at this time of night, especially after the exhausting day she'd had. Coming in and finding a complete stranger sitting at her kitchen table, sharing an intimate meal with her husband, did nothing to improve her mood. "Nice to meet you."

The blonde smiled, her gleaming white teeth glistening under the kitchen spotlights. "Likewise. I hope this is okay? Finding me here in your home at this time of night? I didn't realise it was so late. We got so caught up, bouncing ideas around about how to go forward with the business, that time ran away from us."

Katy fixed a weary smile on her face. "Don't mind me. I'll grab a sandwich and get out of your hair, if you still have business to discuss."

AJ frowned. "I've got your dinner keeping warm in the oven, love. Let me get it for you and you can join us."

"I couldn't eat anything heavy, I just want something light and go straight to bed, AJ. It's been an exceptionally long day. I don't want to appear to be rude but I'm dead on my feet and just need my bed."

Her husband's face dropped, and Lily scraped her chair back and rose from the table.

"I'm so sorry, I don't wish to intrude further. I've outstayed my welcome."

AJ pointed at the seat. "You haven't, Lily, we were on a roll, you must stay."

"Honestly, we'll catch up tomorrow," Lily insisted.

"No, it's fine," Katy said. "Stay, don't mind me. I'll fix

myself a sandwich and let you continue your meeting." Her smile faded a little. She wasn't in the mood to be nice to a stranger in her own home. Not at this hour. What was AJ thinking, inviting her here, knowing that Katy had put in a long day?

"Nonsense, I've got lasagne for you in the oven. It's lovely."

"It was, I can vouch for that," Lily said.

She gave AJ a sickly sweet smile that turned Katy's stomach.

"I said, I'm fine. Don't push the issue, AJ."

He backed away from her, hurt by the way she had snapped at him. "Whatever."

"I really must go," Lily said. "Thanks for the dinner, AJ. I'll be here first thing, just after nine, and we can continue our discussion then. It was nice to meet you, Katy. Again, my apologies for the intrusion, I know what it's like to get home exhausted and... well."

"It's fine. Honestly, stay and continue your meeting. I'll be out of your hair soon enough."

AJ stood there, his head flicking between Katy and Lily, lost for words. Lily left the kitchen, and AJ glared at Katy then ran after her into the hallway.

Katy tried her hardest not to strain her ear to listen to their conversation at the front door. She kicked herself for the green-eyed monster surfacing. That had never happened to her before, and she detested herself for allowing it to come to light now.

The front door slammed, and AJ appeared in the doorway. "How dare you?"

She stared at him, dumbstruck. Finding her voice finally, she said, "I'm sorry. I don't know what came over me."

He marched across the room and gripped the top of her arms. "I have never given you a reason to be jealous, Katy. I love you. I don't have eyes for anyone else. She's a work colleague. If you must know, we spent a lot of time discussing you over dinner."

Katy shook her head. "What? Why? You have no right speaking about me behind my back."

He released her arms and took a step back. It was a good few seconds before he found his voice again. "Why react like that towards her, towards me?"

"Don't do this, AJ. It's been a hell of a day, and I can do without having a blazing row at this time of night. I apologised, let that be the end of it."

"You infuriate me." He stormed out of the room, leaving her to clear up the dishes from the table.

She washed and dried them with tears streaming down her face and then went up to bed. AJ was nowhere to be seen. She tiptoed along the landing and opened the spare room and found him curled up in bed, facing away from the door. "What are you doing in here?"

"Go to bed, Katy. I've had enough for one day."

Katy knew when to retreat. She closed the door softly as tears dripped onto her cheeks. Next, she checked on her daughter in the room across the hallway. Georgie had her arms exposed, and one of her legs was hanging outside the bed. Katy crept into the room and tucked all three of her daughter's cold limbs under the quilt. She swept back a few stray hairs from Georgie's face and kissed her forehead, not once but half a dozen times, needing to feel close or loved by a member of her family. She realised she was being silly; maybe that was the exhaustion playing a part in the way her emotions were all over the place.

Again, she eased the door shut, and with her shoulders slumped went into the main bedroom she usually shared with AJ; however, not that night. Tears misting her vision, she collected a pair of clean pjs from the chest of drawers and stepped into the shower, after which she towel-dried her hair and cursed the fact that she couldn't use the hair dryer before tumbling into bed.

Despite her exhaustion, sleep evaded her for hours, her mind recounting the conversation she'd had with AJ after Lily had left the house, leading her to shed yet more tears. The last time she glanced at the bedside clock it read two thirty-five a.m.

CHAPTER 3

*T*he alarm went off at the usual time of seven the following morning. Katy crept along the hallway and poked her head in on Georgie only to find her in the same position as she'd found her in the evening before, with three limbs exposed. She carried out her motherly duty of tucking all her limbs under the covers again and gently closed the door once more. Turning, she saw AJ standing outside the spare bedroom, his hair messed up and his arms folded in utter defiance. She knew then that she would be leaving home in just over an hour with yet another argument under her belt. She smiled, trying her best to defuse the situation. AJ's arms tightened, and his gaze locked on to hers. It was obvious how livid he still was with her. He held her gaze for several minutes, shrugged, and then went downstairs, leaving her staring after him, wondering if this was the end of her marriage.

While she dressed, she told herself she was being foolish to even consider that. This was a tiny blip in what had been a solid relationship for years. They'd been together around seven years now but only married for just over three. Her heart lay heavy, weighing her down as she descended the stairs to the kitchen. AJ was busy preparing the table for when Georgie woke up.

"Do you need a hand?" she asked.

"Nope. Why now? Why ask today? You usually let me get on with looking after our daughter."

Katy was taken aback by the intensity of his words. Too stunned to reply, she walked across the room and slipped a piece of bread in the toaster. "I'm sorry," she mumbled and shuffled a few steps closer to him.

"For what? Making a show of yourself in front of a guest, my new work colleague, or for not trusting me? The one person who has ever truly loved you. Worshipped the effing ground you walk upon. Which is it, Katy? I'm waiting with bated breath to know."

Katy's eyes squeezed tightly shut, and she bit down on her tongue. With her back turned away from him, she whispered, "I don't want another argument with you, AJ. I've apologised, two, maybe three times now, shouldn't that be enough?"

"Ordinarily perhaps, but this time it's different. I clocked the look in your eye when you saw us together—on opposite sides of the table, I might add. What the dickens you thought we were up to is beyond me. I have never, ever, given you any cause not to trust me, so why now? Why this time?"

"She was in my house. I found her in my house, the two of you together, laughing, enjoying each other's company in my absence, maybe that has something to do with the way I reacted." At that, the toast popped up and startled her. She removed a knife from the nearby cutlery drawer and collected the jar of strawberry jam from the fridge.

"So what? You'd better get used to it—her being here, I mean—because we're going to be working closely together from now on. We weren't socialising when you came in last night, we were discussing work. She has some excellent ideas that I'm keen to incorporate into the business. I can only see our workload getting heavier over the coming months if we start to implement her suggestions. Now, if you've got a problem with that, then we need to sort it out, here and now."

"I haven't. AJ, you have to believe me, I was exhausted last night. On the journey home all I could think about was having dinner in the lounge followed by a snuggle with you on the couch. That went out the window when I found her sitting at the kitchen table, enjoying a meal with *my* husband. Put yourself in my shoes for a moment. How would you feel if the tables were turned and you found me sitting there, laughing with a colleague of the opposite sex?"

He frowned, and his head moved from side to side slowly. "I wouldn't read things into it. I would take the situation at face value, and most of all, I would *trust* you."

Her piece of toast remained untouched on the worktop. She listened to his counterargument, and her heart grew even heavier, if that were at all possible. Shrugging, she glanced into his angry, hurt eyes and said, "I do trust you, implicitly. It was a silly slip-up on my part. Don't continue to punish me for being a momentary idiot, please."

"What's the answer then?"

"To let things drop? Push this all aside and put it down as a mistake of massive proportions by me. Yes, I'm the one in the wrong, I openly admit it."

"At least we agree on something. You know what? I'm more hurt and disappointed at the way you reacted than angry. I thought the one thing we could count on in this life above everything else we have to contend with was each other. I guess I was wrong about that. I need to get our child up, showered and dressed, give her some breakfast, and then take her to school. You see, despite having a full-time job of my own, I still have to find the time to care for our daughter. Remind me, when was the last time you fed our child a single meal? Took her to school? Can you remember where the school is even? It doesn't matter, I'm done arguing. I have a busy day ahead of me, I need to keep my mind clear of anxiety, and arguing the toss with you right now isn't going to allow that to happen."

He marched out of the room, leaving Katy staring after him, her mouth gaping wide open.

Her eyes burned and pricked with unshed tears. She fetched a glass from the cupboard, filled it with cold water from the dispenser in the large fridge and downed it. Then, rather than stand there, waiting for AJ to appear for round two, she picked up her keys, slipped on her coat and shoes and quietly left the house. Before she got in the car, she glanced up at her daughter's bedroom to see the curtains still closed.

Am I doing the right thing? Upping and leaving like this without writing a note, apologising yet again for the way I've screwed up? No, it's better if I walk away now and suffer the consequences later, whatever they might be. Maybe I'll give him a call during the day to pave the way for my return home this evening.

Either way, Katy was aware she was going into work early, but the alternative wasn't something she relished. During the journey, she flicked through the channels on the radio and stumbled across one playing 'Three Times A Lady'. It was the first song they'd danced to as a married couple at their wedding, and instead of making her smile with happiness, the damn tears began flowing once more.

After twenty minutes, she arrived at the station. Katy wiped her eyes and blew her nose several times and then left the car. She drifted through the reception area, relieved that the desk sergeant was busy dealing with a member of the public, too tied up to hold his usual chirpy morning conversation with her. Katy raced up the stairs, collected her first cup of coffee of the day and headed for the office. Not in the mood to combat the mountain of post she found there, she sat behind her desk and simply stared at the wall ahead of her, her mind back at home. Several sips of coffee later, she gave herself a good talking-to, which did the job and put her mind back on the task at hand. Thirty minutes later, she was still only halfway through the mail when there was a knock at the door and Charlie poked her head into the room.

"Blimey, you must have got up early. Couldn't you sleep?"

"Something like that. Make me a coffee, and we'll have a quick chat while I finish dealing with this lot."

"Sounds ominous. Coming right up. Shall I see if I've got a shortbread tucked away in one of my drawers, too?"

Katy smiled. "That would be wonderful. I somehow managed to skip breakfast this morning."

"That's not like you. I'll be back in two shakes of a lamb's tail."

Katy smiled and nodded. She set her mail to one side and booted up her computer, letting out an exasperated groan, seeing what awaited her there.

Charlie entered the room with two mugs and a packet of her favourite biscuits.

"You're the best partner an inspector could ever wish to have. How did it go last night? With the friend, Dawn, wasn't it?"

"Oh, I kind of presumed you would be the one to speak first. Okay, if you insist. Dawn was utterly shocked and appalled by the loss of her best friend. I had to ring another family member to come and sit with her, which meant I was with her for over an hour in the end."

"Ouch, so sorry, Charlie, you could have done without

having to contend with that at that time of night. Did you manage to glean anything of importance from her?"

"Not really. She told me that Paula used to hang out with a group of students at uni, often went for a drink after class."

"And they reckon it's all work and no play being a student these days. By the sounds of it, it's one big piss-up, as usual. Did you ask if she'd been involved in any negative incidents lately?"

"I did, and Dawn couldn't recall anything as such. She said she was reasonably happy at home, the odd argument here and there like most couples, but nothing too detrimental that could warrant her husband wanting to kill her."

"What about the suicide angle, did she have any views on that?" Katy took a sip from her fresh cup of coffee and savoured the taste after her first cup had gone cold beside her.

"She was astounded, said it was inconceivable for her to even consider Paula taking her own life."

"Which matches what her husband and parents told us. Anything else worth noting about her character et cetera?"

"No, nothing really. Although I was there over an hour, she spent most of the time too distraught to speak. It wasn't until her sister showed up that she really found her voice, and then there was no stopping her. She told me she found it hard to believe that someone would hate her so much that they would kill her."

"Okay, that seems fair enough. Thanks for going out there, Charlie, it saved me a trip. Although, I have to say, it would have probably saved me a lot of grief if I had visited the best friend instead of you."

Charlie picked up her cup and cradled it between her hands. "Am I supposed to know what that means?"

"Trouble at home last night. I thought it would blow over this morning, however, I was wrong."

"Sorry to hear that, Katy. Not wishing to be nosey, but you can bend my ear anytime you like, you know that."

"I know. Let's just say at the moment I truly despise myself for the way I kicked off."

"About what?"

Katy glanced at her mug and blew on it to make her coffee ripple. "Okay, I'll tell you, but it remains in this room, between us."

Charlie's brow knitted together. "But of course. I would never betray a confidence. I would hope you'd know that by now."

"I do. I'm sorry, I didn't mean to offend you. That's my problem lately, causing offence to the ones who mean the most to me, and yes, I count you as one of those." She let out a sigh and took another sip of coffee to wet her dry mouth. "I did a stupid, naïve thing last night which is still making me feel physically sick this morning."

"Now you're worrying me. You didn't hurt someone last night, did you?"

"You could say that. It was unintentional. Shit! I'm breaking out in a sweat just thinking about it." Katy wiped her hands on her trousers and then gripped her mug again.

"I can't help you if you don't tell me what's going on."

"I'm getting to it. I got home last night to find another woman in my house." Katy paused to gauge Charlie's reaction to the announcement. There wasn't one, not as such.

"Go on."

"I heard laughter as I entered the front door and drifted into the kitchen to find AJ having dinner with this woman. A young blonde woman, I hasten to add."

"And? What does the colour of her hair have to do with anything?"

Katy chewed on her lip. "It shouldn't, but it was like a red rag to a bull for me. I let fly."

"I don't understand. What did you actually see? AJ in a clinch with this woman, snogging her face off?"

Katy shamefully shook her head. "No," she muttered releasing a heavy breath.

"Then what? I'm struggling to get my head around this."

"They were laughing. She was sitting at my kitchen table with my husband, enjoying herself while my sick child was upstairs in bed."

"Wait, I didn't know that Georgie hadn't been well, why didn't you tell me?"

"Umm... she's fine. I meant she has a heart defect and she shouldn't be subjected to anything like this."

"Like what? I still don't get what you're upset about. Surely you don't suspect AJ of having an affair, do you?"

Katy kept her focus on her mug, fearing that if she glanced up at her partner, she would break down once more. "I don't know."

"Jesus, you didn't come right out and say it, not to AJ, did you?"

"Umm... I might have said something along those lines. God, don't hate me, it's enough that he hates me right now, without adding you to the mix as well."

"All right, you're going to need to back up a little first. Who was she?"

"His new assistant." Charlie let out a high-pitched laugh. Katy stared at her, incensed. "What's so funny about that?"

"Are you for real? Okay, I don't mean to appear to be rude, but you're not thinking rationally about this, not one iota. Do you really think if AJ had either the time or the inclination to have an affair behind your back, he would dare to ask the woman to join him for a meal at your *home*?"

Katy's eyes flickered shut. *Why the fuck hadn't that dawned on me last night?* She opened them to see Charlie smiling broadly at her. "Don't! I can tell you're enjoying this."

"I'm not, I swear. However, experience has told me, even at my tender age, to take a step back and assess things for what they are and not what you perceive them to be at first glance. I know AJ well enough to know that he would never dream of cheating on you, Katy. He adores you and the setup you have."

"Now you're just making me feel guilty about the whole episode."

"And rightly so, in my eyes. You must be crazy to think he would ever look at another woman when he clearly loves the bones of you and Georgie. Christ, do you actually realise how lucky you are to have a man like that in your life? The minute you had Georgie, he took over all the childcare responsibilities and gave up his own career, for fuck's sake."

Katy released her hold on the mug, placed her hands over her ears and shouted, "Stop it. I've heard enough." She lowered her hands to the desk once more and shook her head. "I've been a first-class dickhead, haven't I?"

Charlie chuckled. "I shouldn't need to be the one to point that out to you, but yes, I agree. Jesus, if I were in your shoes, I'd go straight home and plead for forgiveness."

"I can't do *that*."

"You mean your pride won't allow you to do it. Bloody hell, Katy, your irrational reaction to this situation could mean the end of your marriage, and you're allowing your damn stubbornness to stand in the way of putting things right."

Katy was lost for words. She sat there for a while just looking at Charlie, her mind whirling. "You reckon?" she managed to utter a few moments later. "What have I done?"

Charlie reached out a hand to cover hers. "It's not too late, not if you're prepared to do something about it now. If, however, you decide to leave things until you get home tonight, it's only going to make it more awkward for both of you. I'm going to leave you to it." Charlie rose from her chair and headed for the door.

"Will you fill the rest of the team in on the case? I shouldn't be too long."

"Of course I can. At least, I'll do my best. I doubt if I'll be as good as you out there but I'm willing to give it a shot. You do what you need to do. Good luck." With that, Charlie left the room.

Katy didn't immediately dive for her mobile to make the call; instead, she ran through what she wanted to say to AJ several times in her head first. She broke out in a sweat at the prospect of losing him. Charlie was right, it was now or never to fix things.

His mobile rang and rang. She was about to give up when he finally answered the call.

"Hello, Katy. What do you want?" His tone was one of concern rather than having any hint of aggression to it.

"Are you all right?"

"Fine. And you?"

"Where are you?"

"I'm in the car. I've dropped Georgie off to playschool, now I'm on my way to price up a job for one of the parents. Why?"

"Are you alone?"

He groaned. "What sort of question is that? Of course I am."

"I didn't mean anything by it, I was wondering, that's all. I umm…"

"You what? Can you get on with it? The traffic is a nightmare around here, and talking to you is only going to distract me."

"Oh, I see. Okay, I can leave it until later. Yes, I'll do that, we'll chat this evening."

"If that's what you want to do. Who am I to argue with you when your mind is made up?"

She flinched at the harshness that had appeared in his voice and sucked in a calming breath before she responded. "I'll see you later. Have a good day, AJ."

"I will. You, too. Oh, and Katy?"

"Yes."

"I love you more today than I've ever done, and you blowing everything up out of proportion last night may have taken the shine off my evening, but it didn't change anything between us."

She let out the breath she'd been holding in, and the tears surfaced once more. She was an emotional wreck and she'd brought about the problem herself. Regret rippled through her like a shock wave. "I love you, too, and I'm sorry... for not trusting you."

"We'll discuss the ins and outs of what happened later. I really have to go now, love. I'm glad you rang me and didn't let things fester. I fear that might have been too damaging to even contemplate."

"I agree. Good luck with your meeting. I'll pick up something special for dinner, if you like?"

"I'll do it. I'll probably have more time than you during the day anyway. Have a good one."

"I will. See you later." Katy ended the call, her mood far more settled than when she had picked up the phone to make the call.

She finished her drink and drifted into the incident room to find Charlie at the head of the room, going over the events of the previous evening and the rest of the team attentively listening to what she had to say. The whiteboard had been filled out proficiently by her partner. Katy smiled and nodded at Charlie who rounded the meeting up by dishing out the necessary instructions to the team in order to advance the investigation.

Their colleagues turned their chairs around and got on with their work. Charlie stepped forward to speak with Katy.

"How did it go?" Charlie whispered.

"Better than anticipated. He was glad I rang. You were right, it's far better to sort things out early than let things tumble out of control."

"There you go, I can add another string to my bow now, marriage counselling. Maybe not, considering I've recently broken up with Brandon."

They both laughed.

"But you have a new fella waiting in the wings, you can ensure things remain on the straight and narrow with him, can't you?"

"If it goes further than first base. We'll see tonight, we have our first official date."

"Oh wow, how cool. I bet the nerves are jangling, aren't they? I remember going on my first date with AJ. Yeah, maybe we shouldn't go over that, not right now."

Charlie picked up on the fact that Katy blushed and laughed. "I can imagine how the night ended." She wagged her finger. "Naughty you."

Katy grinned and shrugged. "We knew we were right for each other. There was no going back after that night either."

Tutting, Charlie shook her head in disgust. "I don't get you. Why the heck did you overreact last night, knowing how much AJ loves you?"

Katy wrinkled her nose and chewed on her bottom lip. "Because I'm a bloody idiot, that's why."

"No shit, Sherlock. The trouble is, most people don't realise what they've got until it's gone. Don't be one of those people, Katy. I only know AJ a little, but from what Mum told me about him, he gave up far more than his career to be with you. Maybe consider that before you fly off the handle in the future."

"He did, and I will, thank you, wise lady. Okay, setting my personal life aside, we should get down to business. I think we should head back to the uni and have a word with the dean."

CHAPTER 4

*T*hey arrived to find the route into the car park cut off. They managed to find a parking space close to the building that a car had just vacated.

"That's going to be a bugbear for some of the students, having to walk to uni rather than be able to drop their car off a few feet from the main building," Charlie said.

Katy laughed. "We all know how ticked off students can get when they need to use their legs for walking."

"Ouch! I suppose."

Katy got out of the car and glanced over her shoulder at a few SOCOs still at the scene, along with a couple of uniformed officers manning the cordon. On the nearside of the tape were a group of students, who, to be fair, only remained in the area for a few minutes, probably because the weather was a true winter's day that would freeze the brass balls off a monkey and they couldn't be bothered to wrap up warm enough to combat the vile weather.

They entered the main building and seeing a sign indicating the reception area, they set off in that direction. The hallway opened out to a large seating area, and just beyond was a screened office with a couple of women busy shuffling papers. One of the women approached. She slid her spectacles off her face and slotted them into her maroon-coloured, shoulder-length hair.

Smiling, she asked, "Hi, how can I help you?"

Katy and Charlie flashed their warrant cards.

"DI Katy Foster and DS Charlie Simpkins from the Met Police. Would it be possible to speak with the dean?"

"Oh my. Is something wrong?" She waved a hand. "Oh, ignore me, I shouldn't have asked, given what's going on outside. Of course you would show up today to speak with Mrs Johnson."

Katy smiled. "Yes, it's to do with what happened in the grounds last night. Is she available?"

"She's been expecting the police so told me to clear her diary for this morning. I'll give her a call now."

The woman swiftly returned to her desk and picked up the phone. She turned her back on them to make the call and then returned to collect them moments later. "Will you come to the door at the end? I'll show you the way to her office, it's just up the corridor."

Katy smiled and nodded. She and Charlie joined the woman a few feet away and followed her a short distance up the corridor, stopping outside a door with the dean's name emblazoned on a gold plaque.

The woman leaned in and whispered, "Just so you know, Mrs Johnson was devastated to learn of the news last night. She couldn't come yesterday because she was at a dinner party and had been drinking."

Katy cocked an eyebrow and whispered back, "Thanks for giving us the heads-up. What you're telling us is that she might be a little hungover."

"Oh, no… I wasn't suggesting that at all," the receptionist blustered, her cheeks heating up under Katy's intense gaze.

"It's fine, your secret is safe with us."

Before the woman could answer, she was summoned into the room by the dean. She opened the door and shuffled to one side. "Mrs Johnson, this is Inspector Foster and Sergeant Simpson. I think I got that right, didn't I?"

Charlie smiled. "It's Simpkins, but I answer to just about anything most days."

"I apologise. I'll leave you to it. Sorry, can I get anyone a drink?"

"I'm fine," the dean replied. She motioned for Katy and Charlie to take a seat in front of her.

"Not at the moment, but thanks for the offer," Katy replied.

The receptionist closed the door behind her when she left.

Katy and Charlie settled into the chairs ahead of them.

"Thanks for seeing us at such short notice. Sorry you're having to deal with the incident that took place in the university grounds," Katy said. She offered a weak smile.

Mrs Johnson's head slowly moved from left to right. "I'm utterly devastated by what has taken place. I stopped off at the scene on my way in this morning, but no one would tell me anything, said it wasn't their place to fill me in. Which is fair enough, I suppose. So I'm still very much in the dark as to what happened. Saying that, I'm aware of the victim's name. Paula Lowe, is that correct?"

"It is. When we arrived last night, we found the young woman's body at the base of the building closest to the car park. At first glance, the pathologist led us to believe that Paula had taken her own life—that was until she discovered a few marks on Paula's neck. We're awaiting the results of the post-mortem which should come through in the next day or so to confirm if we're dealing with something more sinister."

Mrs Johnson's hands slapped against her cheeks. "Really?

How awful. We haven't had many suicide attempts on campus over the years, or deaths come to that. Although, at other universities throughout the UK, during the pandemic the suicide rate went up. I'm proud to say that we've never experienced anything like this during my term as dean. It's rocked my world and shaken me up good and proper."

"Sorry to hear that, Mrs Johnson."

"Please, call me Fiona. I simply can't believe this has occurred, and to Paula of all people."

"You knew her personally?"

"Yes. Well, I suppose I know her parents more than her, but it amounts to the same thing really. We show up at the same social events occasionally. I gave them a call the second I heard it was Paula who'd lost her life last night. Denise was utterly distraught, too upset to speak with me, and Lesley wasn't fairing much better, I can tell you. I didn't take up too much of their time, I didn't want to intrude on their grief so left them to it. They know they can reach out and speak with me any time they need to. Such a shock to realise their daughter is dead. What do you know about what happened?"

"We can't really go into specific details as yet. Like I said, we're awaiting the results of the post-mortem, and then we can throw everything we've got behind the investigation. So any leads we can source in the meantime could be crucial to how the case proceeds."

"I see, I think. Are you keeping the verdict open, is that what you're telling me? Whether it was suicide or if her death was caused by someone else?"

"Let's just say that we're looking into both prospects at the same time, just to confuse matters."

"It must be tough for you. I suppose keeping your options open makes a lot of sense. How can I help, or is that a silly question?"

"Not at all. What we need is any background information you have regarding Paula's time at uni."

Fiona inclined her head. "Meaning what?"

"Did she come to you with any real concerns? Either about her coursework or any problems with any of the other pupils?"

"No, our paths have never crossed in that respect. You're aware that she was one of our older students, I assume?"

"Yes, did that cause her or any of the other students in her lectures a problem? Is that what you're implying?"

"No, nothing of the sort. All I'm saying is that for some, being an older student in class can seem problematic to the other students. In my experience, the age difference between the students can have a detrimental effect on how the older student performs. It can cast doubts in their minds whether they are up to the task or not."

"Ah, yes. Was that the case with Paula?"

Fiona hitched up her right shoulder and let out a sigh. "I can't say I noticed. She used to hang around with a group of students. From what I could tell, they all appeared to get on well together."

"Can you give us the names of the students?"

"I can put a list together, yes." She scribbled down a couple of names and stopped to consider the rest. "I'm sorry, my head is full of rubbish right now."

Katy thought back to what the receptionist had let slip, that the dean had been socialising the night before and smiled. "There's no rush. Maybe come back to it in a moment. What we're really here for is to see if you would allow us to view the security footage from any cameras in the area of the incident."

"Golly, yes. I wondered if you would want to see them. I can get onto Jack, he's our head of security, he can deal with that for you. Do you want me to do it now?"

"That would be great. Thank you."

She dialled a number and spoke to the security guard. "Jack, it's Dean Johnson. I have a couple of police officers with me. They're going to need you to sort out the security footage you have for around the time the incident took place last night. Shall I send them over to see you...? Okay, we'll finish up here, and I'll bring them over to you in fifteen to twenty minutes. Thanks." She ended the call and wrote another name down on the list. "He's going to get the relevant discs sorted out for you. He's a good bloke. Just tell him if there's anything else you're likely to need, and I'm sure he'll be able to sort it out for you. Oh, yes, there's another one for you." She added yet another name.

"Thanks, it all helps. What type of student was Paula?"

"Very good. Her grades were exceptional in her second and third terms, not so great in the first term because I think she found it all a bit too traumatic being back in the classroom since her school days."

"I think I would feel the same, but she wasn't that old, was she?"

Fiona tapped her keyboard and then ran her hand across her computer screen. "No, she was only twenty-six. I wasn't sure if she was a bit older. Blimey, that's shocked me. What her parents must be going through is... unthinkable, I suppose. I'm willing to work with you as much or as little as you want, Inspector. None of this makes sense to me, but I enjoy solving puzzles. Damn, I didn't mean to make light of the situation."

"I didn't take it as that. Would it be possible to speak with her lecturers while we are here?"

"Oh, yes, anything you need, just shout. I'm missing one name off my list now; who the devil is it? Ah, yes, that's him. Here you go, there are six people in total."

"That's amazing, I doubt if my head at school could have

recalled all the names in a certain group like you have, I'm very impressed with your knowledge."

"It's only because I took an interest in Paula and her stay with us. I just wish for her parents' sake that I had kept a closer eye on her. Maybe if I had, she would still be with us today."

"You can't keep an eye on folks twenty-four-seven, Fiona."

"In reality, I know that, but it won't prevent me feeling a failure. I never like to let a student down, and this tops the lot, doesn't it? When someone loses their life on campus. Shocking, truly and utterly shocking state of affairs. Going back to you covering all the bases, I would be even more appalled to know that Paula was killed by someone on site."

"Hopefully we'll garner enough evidence from the CCTV footage to set the ball rolling one way or another. If it turns out that she ended her own life, then our investigation would draw to a halt swiftly."

"Let's hope that's the case, although I have to be clear and say she always came across as a lovely girl who had her head screwed on properly. I never caught her contemplating life when I spotted her around the campus. We would bump into each other now and again, and she always seemed cheerful enough, especially recently. Therefore, I assumed things were on the right track and going well for her. Which makes no sense at all, does it?"

"Exactly. The more we hear things of that nature, the more inclined we are to believe that we're dealing with a murder inquiry, not wishing to alarm you."

"You can't shock me any more than I am already. It's the not knowing, isn't it?"

"It always makes it more challenging for us, that's for sure. Is there anything else you can think of about Paula that might help us?"

"Such as?"

"Has she ever had to complain about another student coming on strong, badgering her, that type of thing?"

"Nothing at all. I'll check her file just in case I've forgotten anything." Fiona looked at the screen and sighed. "Nothing noted down on her file at all."

"Not to worry. We'll have to see what the CCTV footage comes up with. How many lecturers did she have in total, can you tell us that?"

"Let me bring up her course schedule." A few taps on the keyboard later, and she said, "Four in total. Would you like me to note them down for you?"

"Perfect. Will it be possible to have a quick chat with them today? If it's not too much of a disruption for you all."

"Too bad if it is. Like you said, it's important for you to get this investigation underway, and quickly. I'll send each of them a text message and make the arrangements and then I'll take you over to the security building, it's out the back."

Katy smiled appreciatively. "You're very kind, thank you."

The room fell quiet, except for the sound of Fiona tapping out a message and receiving four responses, one after the other. "They've all said they'd be willing to have a chat with you when necessary."

"It's going to be difficult to arrange, our priority right now is going over the CCTV footage. We could see about fitting in the interviews after that, I suppose. Would that be okay? If we got back to them later?"

"I'll let them know the order of events. I can't see any one of them having any objections. They're all really cut up about the news. We had a brief chat in the staffroom before lectures began this morning. I felt it necessary to make them all aware of what was going on first thing."

"Quite right. Is it possible for us to make our way over to the security building now?"

"I'll take you myself." Fiona left her desk and slipped on a black woollen coat, appropriate for the weather, Katy thought.

Together, the three of them sped through the quiet corridors, out of the main entrance, and dipped around the corner to a small two-storey building.

Inside the front door lay three options to take.

"It's this door here," Fiona said.

She knocked, and almost immediately, a man in his fifties or sixties with greying hair and a beard opened the door.

"Ah, there you are, Jack. This is DI Foster and DS Simpkins. I'll leave them in your capable hands. Show them what they need to see, if you will?"

"I've got the discs set up, Dean Johnson."

"Good. I would stay but I have a Zoom meeting in ten minutes that I really can't miss. We tried to rearrange once we knew you were coming, however the other party was having none of it."

"There's no need for you to stay," Katy told her. "Thanks for all your help so far."

"Not at all, it's been my pleasure. I hope I've been of some hel"

A young man burst into the hallway. He seemed flustered. "Jack, you've got to come with me."

"What's going on?" Jack and Fiona asked in unison.

Katy sensed something terrible had happened.

"It's another... I mean, I've found one of the students... umm, dead."

CHAPTER 5

"What? Where? Take us there, now," Katy demanded, interrupting the conversation between the dean and Jack.

The younger man ran a hand through his hair and spun on his heel. The four of them joined him outside, and they raced around the corner to a bank of temporary garages.

"She's in there. I found the engine running. I didn't touch anything, I left everything as it was. I hope I did the right thing?"

"You did, Eric. Don't worry, the police will handle it now," Jack assured his colleague, patting him on the back between the shoulder blades.

"Charlie, I'll take a look," Katy said. "Call the station, get a team of uniformed officers out here ASAP."

Charlie nodded and stepped away from the rest of the group to make the call. Katy withdrew a mask from her pocket and entered the garage. The fumes were impossible to ignore and affected her eyes in no time at all. She got close enough to the driver's door to view the occupant of the vehicle. She was a young girl, in her late teens or early twenties.

Katy removed a plastic glove from her other pocket and tried to open the door, but it was locked.

Shit! We're going to need to break the glass to get in.

She ran out of the garage and immediately dialled a number on her mobile. "Sorry to trouble you, Patti, it's Katy. I'm at the university. I've just been alerted to another possible suicide. The thing is, the young woman is in a car, and it's running. The car is locked. I thought about breaking the window but didn't want to tamper with it in case it's a crime scene. Any suggestions?"

"We'll deal with the consequences afterwards. If there's a chance she's alive, you need to get into the vehicle, Katy. I'll assemble a team and come out there straight away."

"Thanks, Patti. I'll do what I can."

"Good luck. See you shortly. Stay calm."

"I'll try."

The young security guard had been earwigging her conversation and darted to the side of the garage. He came back with half a brick that had a jagged edge. "Do you want me to do it?"

Katy smiled and nodded. "I hate to say this, but we need the break to be as clean as possible to preserve the scene."

"I've seen a mate do it before, leave it to me." Eric entered the garage and covered his nose and mouth with one arm while he bashed the window with the jagged edge of the brick. After several attempts, the window shattered. He bashed at it some more and made a hole big enough to get his hand through the gap, nicking his flesh in the process. "Damn, I'll worry about that afterwards." With the glove Katy had supplied, he turned the key in the ignition, and the engine died quickly.

Relieved, Katy applauded Eric. "Well done. Can we get the door open?"

He pushed a button on the arm of the door, and the locks

clunked. Katy took a step back to allow the door to open in the confined space.

Eric worked swiftly. He checked the girl for a pulse. "I can't find one."

"Let me see if I can find it."

They swapped places, but Katy's heart hit rock bottom when she realised all of their efforts were in vain. She backed away and looked Eric in the eye. "Thanks for all your help, we were too late."

The pair of them left the garage to find Jack comforting a distraught Fiona.

"I'm sorry, she's gone," Katy said.

Fiona sobbed, and Jack looked beside himself. He tried his best to comfort the dean but couldn't be more distressed himself. Katy took over from him, and he stepped back, shaking his head while Eric flung an arm around his shoulder. The older man shrugged it off.

"I'm fine." Jack said. "It's Dean Johnson we need to worry about, she shouldn't be here, she should be inside."

Katy got the impression he was the type of person who always put others' needs before his own. "That's a great idea. We'll put the footage on hold for now and come back to it later. Let's get Dean Johnson inside, away from here. This place will be swarming with techs and uniformed police soon enough. We'll need to set up another cordon," she said, the last part thinking aloud.

Jack instructed Eric to stay there while he accompanied the dean back to her office. The poor woman was utterly distraught. Charlie came to stand beside Katy, and they both stared at the garage.

"What the actual fuck?" Charlie whispered.

"Exactly. I'm getting another bad feeling about this one. I caught a glimpse of the pedals. There was a brick placed on the accelerator. I'll have to check with Patti, see if that's the norm with a suicide of this nature, but it doesn't seem right to me, not at all."

"I'm with you in that I think it seems odd. Maybe that's what people do, though. If they're unconscious, their foot would fall off the pedal, wouldn't it? Using a brick to hold down the accelerator would ensure the person trying to carry out the act would succeed, surely?"

"Maybe. I've never really analysed this type of thing before. You might be onto something. Damn, I forgot to ask the dean if she knew who the victim was."

Eric was still lingering, listening to the conversation. "I know who it is."

Katy raised an eyebrow. "You do?"

Charlie flipped open her notebook and poised her pen ready to take down the name.

"She's Tina Webster."

Something jabbed Katy's stomach to know more. "Do you know all the names of the students, Eric?"

He smiled and shook his head. "No, only the ones I like. Most of them can't be bothered to give you the time of day around here. They're always looking down their noses at me, but certain ones, like Tina here, well, she was different. Same with the other girl, the one who died yesterday, Paula. She was nice, too."

"Did they hang around together?"

"Yes, there's a group of seven of them, four girls and three lads. Or there were. Now two of the girls are dead."

Katy suddenly remembered the list the dean had given her. She fished it out of her pocket, and there, at the very top, was Tina's name. "Jesus, he's right. I forgot about this. We need to have a chat with the others, and quickly."

"You think someone has it in for the group and is bumping them off one by one?" Charlie asked.

"Possibly. The evidence is leading us in that direction, don't you think?"

Charlie glanced around her. "Maybe. What do you need me to do?"

"Can you go back to reception and see if you can track down the rest of the students? We need to gather them together, if only for their own safety. Plus, we're going to need to ask Dean Johnson to contact the parents of the victim, Tina Webster. See if she can get them to come here. We're going to be snowed under, interviewing the professors and the group of friends, but if the parents can come here, that'll ease our burden. Don't let her tell them over the phone, though, we'll, or should I say I'll, do that when I meet with them. I'll wait here until Patti and her team arrive, they shouldn't be too long."

"I'll see what I can do." Charlie walked back towards the main building.

Katy noticed that Eric was still loitering close by as if he wanted to add to what he'd already told them. "Did you want to say anything else, Eric?"

"Not really. Just that… neither of the girls deserved to die. Had I been in the area, I would have tried to save them."

"I'm sure you would have, you mustn't blame yourself." Katy sensed there was more to Eric than had first met the eye. "Do you want to talk about it, Eric? It might help you deal with your grief better."

"No, I don't think so. I need to get on, Jack will string me up if his instructions aren't carried out by the time he gets back."

He scurried away before Katy had the chance to change his mind. She paced the area for the next few minutes until a couple of patrol cars arrived. She gave them orders to set up a cordon around the garages, and not long after, Patti and her team of techs joined them.

"How's it going, Katy?" Patti jumped out of her van and immediately opened the back doors to obtain her protective clothing. "I suppose there's no point you putting yours on, as you've probably contaminated the scene already."

"You suppose right. Although, in my defence, I did call you before I went in there."

"I know you did, I'm just teasing. Waste of time in the end, was it?"

"Yep, she was already dead. I'm not up to scratch on what happens with suicides of this nature, maybe you can help. I spotted a brick on the accelerator, is that common?"

"A brick, a heavy book, a piece of metal wedged up against it, all of the above. Take your pick. In other words, yes, it's common."

"Yeah, Charlie said the same, it's not something I've really thought about before, that's all."

"Now you know. I'll get a mask on, there are bound to be fumes lingering in there, if you've not long turned off the engine."

"There are."

Instead of Patti pulling on a normal mask, she opted for a heavy-duty gas one.

Katy laughed. "Blimey, that's a bit over the top, even for you."

"No, it's not. Carbon monoxide fumes can be very harmful to one's health, in case you hadn't noticed."

Katy rolled her eyes. "Yeah, what was I thinking? Ignore me."

"With pleasure. Are you coming in with me? If so, there's a mask on the left if you want to grab it."

"Thanks. I was going to ask if you had a spare."

"Saved you the bother then, didn't I? Let's get in there, shall we?"

Katy decided it would be better to pull on a protective

suit as well, and once she was dressed, she followed Patti back into the garage.

"Describe the scene to me, I mean, when you arrived."

Katy ran through the events leading up to her arrival and what had happened when Eric smashed the window to gain entry. All the time Patti nodded, appearing thoughtful, her gaze focused on the vehicle. She inched forward to peer into the car and checked the victim for a pulse.

"There isn't one," Katy said, a little put out that Patti should check.

"Okay, there's no need for you to get your knickers in a twist, it's a matter of course for me, something I do with every victim."

"Really? I never considered it before now."

"You think I'd take a copper's word for it?" Patti peered over her shoulder and grinned. "What type of fool do you think I am?"

"Harsh, Patti. We're supposed to be a team."

"Whatever. You've got your way of doing things and I've got mine. Mine's the right way, always has been and always will be, so there," she added and poked her tongue out.

Katy tapped her foot and let out an exasperated breath. "When you've quite finished. I'd like your expert opinion, if you don't mind."

"I was getting to that. It'll take me a while to check the victim over in such an awkward space."

"I'm not going anywhere," Katy replied. She let out another breath that steamed up the inside of her mask.

Patti laughed. "You might want to control your breathing better in that thing, just a warning."

Katy strode outside, tore off the mask and wiped the inside to ensure the viewing panel was clear again, and then returned to stand next to Patti, who by now was taking photos of the scene from the driver's side while a member of her team was doing the same on the passenger side.

"Any conclusions yet?" Katy dared to ask.

"Patience is a virtue, DI Foster, you should have learnt that by now."

"Cut the crap. I've got two dead bodies on my hands now, Patti, I'm not in the mood for joking around."

Patti took a pace backwards and stared at her. She raised an eyebrow and said, "My, we are touchy today. No, I have no conclusions as yet, nor am I likely to have until I perform the PM later today."

Katy threw her arms out to the sides. "I give up. I should have known that was going to be your response."

"Then why did you ask?"

Recognising there was a battle of wills at play, Katy took the decision to leave the garage without saying another word.

She stripped off her suit, mask and booties and placed them in the black bag close to the cordon. Charlie joined her.

"How did you get on?" Katy asked.

"Are you all right? You look pissed off. Don't tell me Patti has been winding you up again."

"She has, nothing new there. I still reckon she prefers dealing with your mother than with me."

"Now you're just being silly and probably oversensitive."

Katy heaved out a breath. "That appears to be me all over at the moment, doesn't it?"

Charlie nudged her arm. "If you keep thinking that way, then yes, things will always get on top of you."

"That's me told, yet again. Why is it that everyone seems to feel the need to put me in my place all of a sudden?"

Charlie tutted. "We're not, it's a figment of your imagination."

"Maybe. You didn't answer me, how did you get on?"

"Sorry, I've managed to round up all the students. They're waiting to speak with us in a room allocated to us by the receptionist. As to the victim's parents, Dean Johnson managed to call the mother, she was going to contact her husband and come straight here."

"Great. In the meantime, we'll make a start questioning the gang of friends. We can leave them to break the news to the parents when they arrive. Any chance we can grab a coffee on the way? I think I need some caffeine running through my veins before I tackle anything else."

"I took note on the way back, there's a vending machine just inside the main entrance."

"Good."

They headed back to the main entrance and collected a cup of coffee each then continued up the hallway to the room. The students were all standing around chatting to each other. Five of them in total. They stopped speaking the second Katy and Charlie entered the room.

Katy smiled, her gaze scanning the five traumatised faces staring back at her. "Thanks for coming to see us. I'm Inspector Foster, and this is my partner, Sergeant Simpkins. I'm sure you're aware by now of the shocking deaths of two of your friends. What we need to do is question you individually, to see if there's anything you can tell us that will help us determine how Tina and Paula died."

"What?" a young man with spiky red hair said. "Did they commit suicide?"

"Maybe. As with any suicide, we always leave the door open to the possibility that a crime might have been staged to suggest a suicide has taken place. It's what we do."

He glanced at the others and shrugged. "That's news to me."

"Shut up, Boris," one of the girls said. "Does it even

75

matter? The police need to investigate what happened, let them do that without any hassle from us, all right?"

"All right, Heidi, there's no need to speak to me like that. I was just pointing something out. Maybe I should keep my mouth shut instead."

"That would be a grand idea," another of the boys said.

Boris crossed his arms and perched on the desk behind him, glowering at the two people who had spoken out against him.

"All right, guys. I appreciate how upsetting this situation must be for all of you, but falling out with each other isn't going to help, is it?" Katy said. "Why don't we all take a seat? My partner and I will question you all individually. We'll try not to keep you long."

"It's okay, we don't have another lecture now until after lunch, you caught us just finishing up our last lecture, not that any of us could concentrate after hearing the news about Paula first thing this morning, and now Tina has gone, too," one of the other girls said. She wiped away a tear with the back of her hand.

"Why don't I interview you first?" Katy smiled at the young lady. "I'll speak with you three on the right, and my partner will question Boris and you," Katy said, pointing to one of the other boys who hadn't spoken as yet.

"Suits me," Boris shot back. "All right with you, Danny?"

The other boy shrugged.

Katy organised the rest of the group and sat down at the desk. She flipped open her notebook then glanced across to the other side of the room at Charlie who gave her the thumbs-up.

The two girls and boy shuffled together nervously.

"It's okay, there's no need to be scared," Katy assured them. "Why don't you take a seat?" she asked the smaller of the two blonde girls.

She glanced at the other two, who both nodded.

"You'll be fine, Heidi, go on," the other girl said. She gave Heidi a friendly shove towards the chair.

"I'm sorry, I'm well out of my comfort zone, speaking to the police, I've never had to do that before."

Katy smiled to put the girl at ease. "Don't worry, we'll take things slowly, if that's what you want. No pressure from me, I promise."

Heidi sat and blew out the breath she'd been clinging on to. "I'm good. What do you need to know?"

"First of all, I'd like to know how well you knew Paula and Tina."

"We were friends, hung around together all the time we were at university and even socialised at the pub occasionally, after lectures, not that often, granted, because money is tight for everyone."

"And what about last night, where were you?"

Heidi quickly cast a glance towards her friends, and then her gaze fell on her hands that were twisting around a tissue. "We were up on the roof, as usual, then we drifted over to the pub for a quick one."

"The roof? Of the building close to where Paula was found last night?"

"Yes, we left her up there. I was one of the first to leave to go to the pub, I was with Lizzie." Heidi smiled at the other girl waiting to see Katy.

"And how often did you go up on the roof? Was it a regular hangout of yours?"

"Quite often. It's supposed to be out of bounds, but one of the boys got hold of a spare key, and we ended up going up there quite a lot, depending on how good the weather was."

"What did you do up there?"

"Just hung out. Chatting, drinking. It was getting a bit fresh up there last night, I'd forgotten to bring my coat with me, so had Lizzie, so we left earlier than planned and took comfort in the pub instead."

"Any reason why Paula didn't go with you?"

"None that I can think of, unless you count that she seemed to be a little distracted last night."

Katy tilted her head and asked, "Did she say why?"

"No, and I'm not one to stick my nose in where it's not wanted, I have enough shit going on in my own life without being burdened with other folks' problems."

"I see, so you believe she was troubled by a certain problem. Would that be to do with her marriage, do you think?"

"I'm not sure. I suppose the only person who would have the answer to that question would be her husband, Adrian. Have you spoken to him? You must have by now. That's what the police do, speak to the next of kin before they begin their investigation, isn't it?"

Katy smiled and nodded. "Yes, that's all done and dusted. He mentioned they had a somewhat fractious marriage at times."

"That's an understatement, if Paula's recent moods were anything to go by."

"Do you believe she was contemplating ending her life?"

"Nope, I would never have said that, maybe her marriage, but not her life. Why would she? She was doing really well in her lectures. Being here was going to allow her to make a new life for herself. To walk away from her marriage and get a new career where she didn't have to rely on her husband."

Katy jotted the information down. "And she told you this?"

"Not directly, but we could all see the determination in her once she entered her lectures. She was so focussed, every professor we met called her a human sponge, soaking up all the information."

"Isn't that normal? Doesn't everyone gather the information in the same way?"

"No, not really. There are some students I could name who are only here because their parents insisted they should come to university, probably to get out of their hair at home."

Katy raised an eyebrow. "I've never even considered that prospect before. I always got the impression that most parents hated the thought of their children leaving home."

"Some of them, maybe. Mine preferred me to stay local, that's why I stuck with going to a uni locally. You should see the distance some of the students have had to travel to come here. There are several from Newcastle, one or two even from as far away as Edinburgh in some of my lectures. My mother would throw a wobbly if I attended a uni miles away, not to mention the costs involved in forking out for accommodation et cetera. Much easier and cheaper to remain at home and attend this uni. It was a no-brainer for me and Mum to consider."

"It's always struck me as odd, teens moving so far away from their parents just to attend uni. I'm aware that some universities are more prestigious than others, but it's still often struck me as odd, nonetheless."

"It's the way of the world, I guess. The UK copying the US in something yet again. Most kids opt to move far away to attend uni from what I can tell."

"Anyway, moving on… Did Paula ever indicate any suicidal tendencies at all?"

"No, that's why I was so shocked when I heard the news this morning. I was totally bummed when Boris told me first thing, and now we have Tina's death to deal with as well."

"The same question regarding Tina: did you pick up anything untoward with her?"

"No, again, nothing. They both seemed really happy, but

then, who can tell these days? People have become clever about hiding their true feelings, haven't they?"

"What makes you say that?"

"Look at the number of comedians who have mental health issues. Robin Williams is a prime example. A pure genius who took his own life in the end, and there are many more people it has happened to as well. Their names escape me at the moment, though."

"You raise a valid point. I know the dean mentioned that statistics for student suicides have been high at other universities since Covid took hold, but she also stated that this university had escaped much of that, and now we're looking at two possible suicides within the space of twenty-four hours."

Heidi frowned and glanced up from her hands. "You said only possible suicides, what do you mean by that?"

"As with any suspicious death we're forced to investigate the alternatives as a matter of procedure. We never take a sudden death on face value. That's why it's imperative for us to do the necessary digging into a victim's background. To see if there was any indication that either of the girls had suicidal thoughts before their deaths."

"Ah, I'm with you now. Well, I can tell you categorically that they didn't have those sorts of thoughts. I'm sure I would have picked up on any huge mood swings that sometimes accompanies mental health issues. I never did. We were together most of the time, either during lectures or afterwards, in a secret place up on the roof or at the pub. Crap, if Paula jumped off that roof, how am I ever going to be able to go up there again? And as for Tina to do that to herself, Jesus, I didn't know she had it in her to carry out something as devious as that. I wouldn't know where to bloody begin, would you?"

"No, not in the slightest. Maybe if we track her laptop down, we'll find a search in her history that might help us."

"Ah, yes, that's a good idea. I wonder if it was in her car with her, it might be the best place to search for it."

Katy raised an eyebrow. "I'll get the SOCO guys to keep their eyes open. As a group, have you ever encountered any trouble from any of the other students?"

"Like a gang warfare type of thing?"

"Is that what you'd class yourselves as, a gang?"

Heidi's eyes screwed up. "Er... now you've come to mention it, no, I don't think so, not really. We were just a group of seven people, hanging out as friends."

"And there was no animosity or any arguments between you?"

Shaking her head, Heidi said, "No, never. Life's too short... what am I saying? I think we all realise now how short it can be. God, I'm really going to miss them both. They had such interesting lives."

"Such as?"

"Well, I suppose Paula's life was less interesting than Tina's really. Paula was married so she brought a lot of insight into what married life was about, but Tina belonged to every club under the sun. It often puzzled me how she found the time to fit us all in while she attended these groups."

"What type of groups? Are we talking study groups?"

"No. Everything from drama to gymnastics, cooking to sewing. She was a dab hand at sewing, there wasn't anything she wasn't good at really. There was talk of her entering that programme on TV, *The Great British Sewing Bee.*" Heidi teared up. "She would have won it, too, hands down. Amazing, she was. She used to work with a drama group and helped make all their costumes for the plays they used to put on. Like I said, I'm not sure how she ever found the time to hang out with us, but she did."

"Such a shame she's no longer with us. I take it she still lived at home?"

"That's right, with her parents. Don't ask me what they're like, I've never met them."

"Was her home life happy?" Katy probed.

"Oh yes, she wasn't the type to ever have a cross word with anyone, let alone her parents. She wanted for nothing in that respect, she was the only one amongst us who had her own car." Heidi fell silent again and shook her head. "I can't believe she would have taken her own life, not like that. She loved that car. Maybe that's the reason she used it to take her life, because she loved it so much. I don't know, I'm guilty of saying whatever comes into my head at the moment, my mind is shot. Nothing is making sense to me. To have lost two friends, both presumed to have committed suicide, within twenty-four hours of each other, it's hard to get your head around something as devastating as that."

"I'm sure it must be. Can you think of anything that we should be checking out?"

"Not off the top of my head. You asked if as a group we had fallen out with anyone, we haven't, so unless you want me to make something up, there's really nothing else I can tell you."

"Okay, what you've told me is a real help, it gives me a bit of an insight into the two girls. Thanks for that. Can you send Lizzie over now?"

"Will do. I hope you figure out what happened soon." Heidi stood and swapped places with Lizzie.

Katy took the chance to see how Charlie was doing on the other side of the room. It looked like she was taking plenty of notes from the guy sitting opposite her.

"Hello, shall I sit down? I'm Lizzie."

Katy smiled at the young woman, noting the sadness looming in her blue eyes. "Please do. I'm Inspector Foster, but you can call me Katy, if you like."

"Thanks. I have to say from the start, I'm not sure I can offer you anything, my head's a mess. I keep reliving our last week together, as a group. Our time spent together was filled with happiness, lots of laughter and tears of the good variety. I can't imagine any of us ever laughing again after what we've learned today. It just doesn't add up at all."

"Are you telling me that neither Paula nor Tina ever spoke to you about ending their lives?"

"Never, not in their wildest dreams. Why would they? They had everything to live for. I don't really want to repeat what you've already been told by Heidi, but they both led really busy lives, too busy to even have the time to contemplate doing away with themselves." She hugged her arms around herself and shuddered. "It doesn't ring true to me at all."

"Try not to get too upset; I know that's easy for me to say. Is there anything you can think of that these ladies said to you over the past few weeks that might lead you to believe something serious was going on in their lives?"

"You mean contemplating suicide again? No. If they had even hinted at it, I would have accompanied them to the uni counsellor. They were their usual happy selves. That's why I'm struggling to get my head around it, why we all are. In fact, I feel physically sick. If I didn't have to be here, talking to you, I'd more than likely be bent over the loo, emptying my stomach. I've never felt this way about someone's death before. A boy I was close to at school got knocked off his bike on the way home one day, we were told about it the next day. Yes, it rocked my world, but my emotions weren't torn apart like they are now, having to deal with this godawful news. One death is bad enough, but two of my friends killing themselves within a day of each other, that's unthinkable to consider. I'm trying my best to block it out, without much success. Why? Why would they?"

"That's why we have to interview you guys. Believe me, I appreciate how difficult this must be for all of you, but unless we delve into each girl's background, we're going to be going round in circles for weeks to come."

"I understand. I want to help you, but I'm not sure I can. They both meant so much to me." Tears dripped onto her cheeks. She wiped them away with her sleeve. "I'm sorry, I've tried my hardest to hold my emotions in check since I heard about Tina…"

"You don't have to apologise. Maybe it would be better if you just let it out."

"Don't give me the green light to do that, I fear I won't be able to turn the tap off once the tears start flowing."

"It must be very hard for you to lose someone so close at your age. Maybe you should seek out some advice from the counsellor before you head home today."

"I will, thanks. Do you need me for anything else?"

"No, you're free to go, if you'll promise me that you'll reach out to someone for help."

"I will. Thanks for not pushing me."

"That's not why we're here. Go back to Heidi. If you can send the young man over…"

"He's called Tyler. He's really cut up about Tina. I think he had a secret crush on her that none of us noticed until today."

"Ah, in other words, you're warning me to tread carefully, I get it."

Lizzie smiled and drifted back to sit with Heidi. She crossed paths with Tyler as he came towards Katy.

"Hi, are you Tyler?"

"Yes, Tyler Dodds."

"Pleased to meet you. This is just an informal chat about Paula and Tina, no pressure at all, so try to relax, if you can."

"Thanks. Heidi and Lizzie have probably told you how gutted we all are to have lost them. There's no reasoning behind why they should have taken their own lives. It's a mystery to all of us, one that we're hoping you can solve quickly. Do you have any idea why they would both want to kill themselves?"

Katy shrugged. "I was hoping you and the others could tell us that. Heidi and Lizzie said that they couldn't think of an occasion when the two girls mentioned something about wanting to end their own lives. How about you?"

He inhaled a large breath and shook his head. "Nope, not a solitary occasion. I would have been there for them, if they had. I went through a similar incident at school when one of my classmates hung himself in the woods. Along with another friend, we were the ones who found him after school one day and called the police. They told us to leave him alone." He fell quiet. "The thing is, he was still moving when we got there, only slightly, but moving all the same. I think we could have saved him. The police took almost twenty minutes to arrive, and by that time… he was dead."

"That must have been very traumatic for you to deal with. I'm sorry about that."

He gulped noisily. "It's in the past. I wish it could have stayed there, too, but all this has brought it flooding back."

"I'm so sorry you're having to deal with this. I promise not to detain you for too long and then you and your friends can go off somewhere to contemplate."

"Will that make things better? I doubt it. What do you need to ask me?"

"How close were you to Paula and Tina?"

"Umm… I suppose I was closer to Tina than Paula, what with her being slightly older and married. Tina and I were the best of friends. We used to attend the same school together. I was relatively shy back then, but when we got to uni I plucked up the courage to speak to her, and then we formed a group with the others."

"Did your friendship develop into anything else?"

"Not really. Although I have to admit I sometimes wished it had. I could never find the courage to ask her. The others used to tease us, and it always forced me back into my shell again, too scared to speak out. I really liked her a lot, not that she had the time to go out on dates or anything like that. She's what my mum would have classed as a social bee, always on the go, buzzing from one thing to the next."

Katy felt sorry for the poor lad, having missed his chance at real happiness by the sounds of it. "I'm so sorry you never got the chance to let her know how you felt."

His head dipped, and he sniffled. "I'll never know if my feelings would have been reciprocated or not. Tina was outwardly friendly to everyone she met. For all I know, if I'd cornered her, so to speak, she might well have slapped me, and that might have been the end of our beautiful friendship."

"And that's why you thought twice about approaching her?"

"Yes, fear of rejection and spoiling the dynamics we had as a group."

"Seems a shame, an opportunity lost that I fear you may regret in the future."

"You've got that right. I know they say life goes on, but does it, really? I feel so raw, I know I'm going to struggle to get my head straight over the coming weeks and months. Neither of them should have gone out that way. They should have confided in us as a group, we could have handled it, worked through things together. Robbing us of the opportunity to help ease their inner turmoil, that's what I'm going to struggle with, I can tell you."

"Did either of the girls ever mention having problems with some other individual at all?"

He inclined his head. "What are you saying? That you think someone killed them, that they didn't kill themselves after all?"

"There's a possibility, one that we need to investigate fully before we close the case as being two suicides."

"God, now I see where this is leading. You don't believe in coincidences, as a copper, do you?"

"That's right, no copper really does. There's always an alternative waiting around the corner to be pounced on."

"Not trying to tell you how to do your job or anything, but I definitely think you should be considering the alternatives because every single one of us is going to tell you the same thing, there's no way on this earth those two girls committed suicide."

"Actually, the others have said the same. We still have the CCTV footage to examine. Hopefully that will give us a few leads to go on. If nothing shows up, then we have zilch to play with. That's why I felt it was important for me and my partner to have a chat with you guys, people who would know them best."

"In the hope we'll be able to fill in the blanks for you, is that right?"

Katy pointed and then tapped the side of her nose with the same finger. "See, we're on the same wavelength after all. Now, can you recall either of the girls falling out with anyone either on or off the campus in the last month or so? Take your time, it could be vital to our investigation."

He did as requested, delayed his response until he'd mulled the question over thoroughly in his mind. "Not really, at least I don't think so. I wish I could think of someone.

Mind you, I'd probably keep the information to myself and go round there and beat seven bells of shit out of them."

Katy tutted and wagged her finger. "Not an appropriate answer, Mr Dodds."

He sniggered. "As if I would, I was only winding you up. In all seriousness, I can't think of anyone. That's not the type of thing any of us would keep to ourselves, if only to safeguard the others, you know, tell them to be on their guard around so-and-so, that type of thing."

"You always looked out for each other, is that what you're saying?"

"Yes, always."

"Were you up on the roof with Paula last night?"

"We all were, until we all started drifting over to the pub across the road. It was cold up there, we didn't stay long. Someone said that Paula was on the phone to her husband and she'd follow us over for a quick one before she went home to be with the miserable git."

"You don't get along with Adrian?" Katy asked, her interest rising a touch.

Tyler stared into the distance behind Katy and chewed his lip. "He's all right, I suppose. I always got the impression that he was a touch envious of her going to uni, or maybe he was jealous, or pissed off even, due to her having late lectures and being unable to have his dinner on the table for when he finished work. I don't know, I'd never go out on a limb and call him a happy chappie, always wearing a soured expression like someone had dumped a load of manure on his car, if you get my drift?"

"I do. Do you think he was capable of hurting Paula?"

"Who can tell these days? If someone is pushed enough, they'll do anything, won't they?"

"Maybe. It's a funny world we're living in."

"In other words, all the compassion people showed

towards each other during the pandemic has gone out of the window now and it's back to normality, right?"

Katy liked this young man, he told it as he saw it. "You have a wise head on your young shoulders, Tyler."

"God, don't you start, my gran always says the same." His cheeks flared.

"Is there anything else you can tell me about either of the victims, sorry, Paula and Tina?"

"Not really, only that they're going to be missed by all of us. The group will never be the same again. What will happen about their funerals?"

"You'll need to keep in touch with the families about those. There will be a slight delay because of the post-mortems and all the tests that will need to be performed before the pathologist signs the bodies over."

Tyler winced.

"I'm sorry, that was too much information for you. Can you call the families without feeling awkward?"

"Maybe not me, but we'll get one of the girls to do it, it might come across better."

"I'll leave that with you. I can have a word with them, to pave the way for you, if you want?"

He smiled. "Would you?"

Katy patted the back of his hand. "No problem. Thanks for speaking with me. You take care of yourself, okay? Be extra vigilant in the coming few days."

"Do you think there's more danger out there?"

"Who knows? Just ensure you and the others remain together and aware of your surroundings, in case."

"We'll stick together as a group, it's all we can do, isn't it?"

"Take care."

He left the table. Katy's gaze wandered across the other side of the room to find Charlie still in deep conversation with one of the boys. She tried to get her attention but couldn't. So Katy remained seated and sifted through her notes, jotting down the more interesting facts that she had gathered.

The door opened a few minutes later, and the receptionist stuck her head into the room. "Dean Johnson wanted me to come and fetch you, tell you that Tina's parents are here."

"Thanks. We're almost finished, we'll be along shortly."

She nodded and left the room again. Charlie rolled her eyes at Katy as if she was having a tough time talking to the young man opposite her. Katy decided to go over and lend her a hand.

"Hi, are we nearly done here?" Katy pulled up a chair and sat close to Charlie. Katy noticed the amount of notes Charlie had taken compared to her.

"Almost, aren't we, Boris?" Charlie said to the young man with red spiky hair opposite her.

"If you think I've given you enough to be going on with, then yes, I think we're done here."

"You've definitely given me more than enough to sift through."

Katy rose from her seat. "Then we should be going."

In the hallway, once Charlie had joined her, Katy asked, "How did it really go in there?"

"The first lad, Danny, couldn't really tell me much, but Boris... let's just say there was no stopping him once he was wound up. I think he was really close to both the victims and was cursing the fact that their young lives had been robbed by 'an evil individual', was how he put it."

Katy sighed. "He's not wrong there. My three were pretty much the same. The two girls were maybe too upset to think of anything to give me, but when I spoke to Tyler, who happened to fancy Tina, even though he didn't come right out and admit it to her, he gave me an insight into what Adrian was like, Paula's husband."

"What? Enough for you to consider putting him in the frame for her murder?"

"Possibly. I'm going to bear him in mind. We'll do the necessary background checks on him just in case. One of the girls also mentioned she thought Paula had gone back to uni to better herself and to give her a foundation for leaving her husband."

"Interesting. I'll have to go over my notes and pull out anything pertinent. The trouble is, Boris rambled on so much, I kind of switched off after a while."

Katy dug her in the ribs. "FYI, that's not how you're supposed to hold an interview. You should be alert and attentive at all times, it says so in the police procedural manual one-oh-one."

"Whatever, I reckon you would have done the same in my situation."

Katy grinned. "More than likely. Straight faces and mind back on business, we've got the parents to deal with now and all the angst that will bring with it. After that, we'll need to return to view the security footage."

"I get the feeling we're going to be stuck here all day."

"Yep, sounds about right. It is what it is. Maybe the dean will allow us to grab a meal in the canteen at lunchtime."

"I wouldn't count on it."

They stopped talking, now that they were only a few feet from Dean Johnson's office. Katy knocked on the door and waited for the dean to invite them in.

"Come in."

Katy held her crossed fingers up. "Hope this goes well, although I sense otherwise."

She opened the door, and she and Charlie entered the room.

A man and a woman, both smartly dressed, occupied the two chairs in front of the dean. To the side were two empty ones, so Katy and Charlie headed for them while the dean introduced everyone.

"And why are we here?" Terrence said. "More to the point, if this has something to do with Tina, shouldn't she be here with us? We tried to call her but her phone went into voice-mail, so we presumed she was in a lecture."

Katy shuffled forward in her chair, the man's abrupt tone already putting her on edge. "I'm sorry to have to inform you that your daughter was found dead this morning."

Terrence leapt to his feet, tipping back his chair. "Don't be absurd. What's the meaning of this, Fiona? What in God's name is this woman talking about?"

His wife latched on to his arm. Sniffling, she pleaded, "Terrence, calm down and let the woman speak."

"Calm down? I've just been told my daughter is dead, and you're sitting there telling me to calm down. Aren't you upset?"

He righted his chair and fell into it.

His wife clutched his hands with both of hers. "I am upset. But I want to hear what the inspector has to say in a calm manner. What use is it to any of us if we fly off the handle? You know what the doctor said about keeping your blood pressure under control."

"Sod him. She's just told us *Tina is dead*, hasn't that sunk in with you yet?"

"Of course it has. I'm still trying to process it while ensuring you remain calm."

He removed his hands from hers and folded his arms across his heaving chest. "Say what you have to say. How did she...?"

"We were already here on campus and were able to attend to the scene quickly. She was found in one of the garages with the engine running. One of the security guards managed to break the driver's window, and we were able to switch off the ignition. It was too late, she'd already gone, I'm sorry."

The couple stared at each other, and Susan Webster whispered, "Suicide? I don't believe it."

"No, neither do I," her husband stated adamantly. "There's no way Tina would have taken her own life, no way, I'm telling you. Solid as a rock in character and everything she did. She had too much to live for. Always on the go, that girl, never sitting still for a minute. She would never contemplate taking her own life, never. I'm as sure about that as I am that the sun rises and sets every day. No way!"

Susan sniffled and removed a tissue from her handbag. "I'm with my husband on that one. She had the world at her feet. She was confident and had a zest for life and any other cliché you want to throw around in that vein. This is... I can't believe this has happened, not to my baby girl. She would have spoken to us. We're aware of the pressures heaped on students' shoulders these days. We sat down at the end of each week and went through any problems she needed help in solving, we both did. We were a very close family, and not once did I get the impression that she wanted to do anything as silly as... this."

"I think you should tell them," Dean Johnson chipped in, her hands intertwined on the desk in front of her.

"Tell us what?" Terrence was quick to pounce.

"Unfortunately, this is the second suicide we've been called out to investigate at the university in the last twenty-four hours," Katy replied.

"What? What's going on here, Fiona? How can you allow this to happen on your watch?"

"Terrence. That's grossly unfair. We all know what an excellent job Fiona does here."

He turned to face his wife. "Do we? How come two kids have lost their lives here in the last few days then? Answer me that!"

The dean raised a hand to prevent the couple from having a go at each other. "Susan is right, you both are. I should have been more vigilant. I'm guilty of taking my eye off the ball. Last night, Paula allegedly threw herself off a building where the students shouldn't have been allowed to congregate. That's down to me. However, in Tina's case, I'm not sure what I could have done to prevent her taking her own life in the manner she did."

"How would my daughter even know where to begin with killing herself in that way? Ah yes, the great invention that is the internet, that's what you're going to suggest, isn't it?" Terrence asked, his eyes blazing as he stared at Katy.

Before Katy could answer, his wife tugged on his arm and whispered, "You're missing the point, she said Paula had died."

"What? Paula Falkirk, I mean Lowe? Jesus, that's another one who I would never suspect had it in her to kill herself, if that's what you're telling us?"

"In Paula's case, we found evidence to suggest otherwise, unlike your daughter's case, although…"

"Although?" Terrence jumped in immediately.

"We're awaiting the results of the post-mortem at the moment. Until we have those, we're going to keep an open mind. In your daughter's case, the position she was found in would prove difficult for anyone to assess the body at the scene. The pathologist is examining the body now."

"I want to see her," Terrence demanded.

"Is that wise?" Fiona asked.

"I'm inclined to agree with the dean, sir. I would advise against seeing her until the pathologist makes the necessary arrangements for you to view her body at the mortuary."

He jumped out of his chair and stormed out of the room. "Try and stop me," he flung over his shoulder then slammed the door behind him.

"He can't go there," Katy seethed under her breath. "It wouldn't be right to see her at the scene. I'm going to have to stop him." She left the room and dialled Patti's number.

It rang several times, then Patti eventually answered.

"I'm busy, Katy. What do you want?"

"I wouldn't interrupt you if it wasn't important. The victim's father is on his way down there. Get the uniformed officers to head him off. I thought it would be quicker to ring you directly rather than go through the station."

"Ah, got you. Okay, I'm on it now. I presume he didn't take it well."

"Nope. Hurry, he should be there soon."

Katy ended the call and returned to the dean's office. "Hopefully, he'll be turned away before he gets the chance to see her. I'm sorry, it's just that we don't allow the victims' families anywhere near their bodies, not at the scene. There are always different tests to conduct, and if we allowed all and sundry to go near the area, we would have a contaminated scene in no time at all, which could be detrimental to the outcome of the investigation."

"I know that, and so does Terrence, or he should," Susan Webster said. "You have to understand how upset he is, how upset we both are. Tina was our only child, and we're both beside ourselves."

"I appreciate that, but our job is difficult enough." Katy left it there when Susan nodded. "You get where I'm coming from. Are you up to answering questions about Tina, Mrs Webster?"

"Like what?"

"I take it from what you've told us already that your

95

daughter has shown no suicidal tendencies in the past few months or so."

"That's correct. We speak to each other frequently, and she never has down days. Always bending our ear about the projects she's working on, very enthusiastic about things actually. Is that how someone would react if they were on the verge of taking their own life?"

"No, not at all. From what Dean Johnson has told us about Paula, the same could be said about her as well. That's what we're struggling to comprehend, as you can imagine. Did she have any friends outside the group she hung around with at uni?"

"Honestly, she had so many friends, coming out of her ears, they were. She was never off the phone. I tell a lie, when she was off the phone, her head was stuck in her books, either doing coursework or arranging something for the drama group she was involved in." She sniffled again and blew her nose on a fresh tissue Fiona had passed her. "I don't know how we're going to cope without her. You've seen how irate her father can get, he was never like that when she was around. He cherished her, we both did. I know every parent is bound to put their child on a pedestal, but in Tina's case, she was a very special young lady. Always keen to put others' feelings first. Never selfish. Even when our business was struggling a few years ago, she wasn't the type to have a childish rant or give us a want list for Christmas. She took it all in her stride and said, 'Just give me what you can afford'. Which wasn't much at the time, but we made up for it when we turned the business around at the end of last year. I think every business took a major hit during Covid. We had to dig deep to remain strong as a family, to get us through it. Luckily, we've come out the other side and the orders are flooding in once more."

"What sort of business do you run?"

"We sell boats, anything from vast yachts for Russian billionaires to small yachts for the novice sailors, and anything in between."

"I'm glad business has picked up again for you. Where are you based?"

"Here in London. I know that sounds daft, but we tried setting the business up elsewhere, however, the logistics didn't work out for us."

"I see. And you work alongside your husband full-time?"

"Yes, it's a joint business. Tina always came along for the ride when we got involved in one of the large shows. She loved interacting with people, that's why she joined the drama club." She covered her face with her hands and cried.

Fiona left her seat and sat in the chair vacated by Terrence moments earlier.

Katy suddenly felt the need to back off. "I'm sorry. If you'd rather we left it there for now, it's fine by me."

"No, I'm sorry. I want to be compliant, help you all I can. I need to get to the bottom of why our daughter did this. It's so hard dealing with the fallout, knowing that she's no longer with us."

"Let's leave it there for now. I'll give you one of my cards. You can ring me day or night if you can think of anything else to add."

Susan took the card and looked Katy in the eye. "If there is anything sinister going on here, please, please do your best to solve it."

"You have my word. Take care. We'll get off and leave you in Fiona's capable hands."

"If you see Terrence, send him back here, will you? Tell him I need him."

"I'll be sure to do that, don't worry. That's providing he'll listen to me, of course," Katy replied.

She and Charlie left the room and walked the length of

the corridor to the main entrance. The area was still and quiet, giving Katy time to reflect on what had been said.

"None of this is making any sense, is it? Two suspected suicides; the jury is still out on the second one until we have another chat with Patti. But both girls had good lives, why would they want to end them?"

"I don't think they did. I know we haven't got much evidence to go on, but to me, both girls knew each other and they've both been found dead in suspicious circumstances."

"It's a tough one to call until Patti can give us a lowdown on what she's found during both PMs. I want to check in with her first, make sure Terrence Webster is behaving himself, and then we'll head over to view the footage. Christ, it's been a long day already, and it's not even lunchtime yet."

"Tell me about it."

Patti was having a heated discussion with Terrence as they rounded the corner to the garages.

Katy groaned and upped her pace. "Just what we don't need. Poor Patti."

"I think she's giving as good as she's getting," Charlie replied.

"She still shouldn't have to contend with that crap, though."

"Granted."

"What's going on here?" Katy stopped alongside Patti with Terrence Webster a few feet away from them and Charlie holding back, assessing if the situation warranted a backup team to attend.

"I demand to see my daughter, and this person," Terrence sneered at Patti, "is preventing me from doing it. Maybe now you're here you can have a word with her, show her the error of her ways."

"I'm sorry, Mr Webster, I won't be doing that. As I told you back in the dean's office, you will have your chance to view your daughter's body once the post-mortem has taken place."

"You mean once she's been cut to pieces and disfigured. I have a right to see her the way she is now. Don't make me go above your head, I have a direct line to the chief constable."

Katy shrugged. "That's your prerogative. Make the call, sir. I'm sure he'll tell you the same as we're telling you."

He threw his hands up in the air and circled the area a few times. Each time he passed either Katy or Patti, his eyes narrowed in a hateful glare. Eventually, after contemplating the rights and wrongs of the situation, he ground to a halt and shouted, "You haven't heard the last of this."

"I'll keep my phone handy at all times, sir, awaiting the chief constable's call."

He huffed out a breath and marched back towards the main building once more.

Katy rubbed Patti's upper arm and asked, "Are you all right?"

"I'm okay. I stood my ground, had my guys on standby in case he kicked off big time. Placing myself in his position, I'm sure I would have done the same if that were my child in there. But there's no way I was going to let him near her. Do you think he was pulling a fast one, mentioning your senior officer?"

"Possibly, I suppose I'll know soon enough. I'll keep my phone handy and my objection well versed in my head."

Patti smiled. "Let's hope it doesn't come to that and that his wife is able to calm him down once he's inside. I'd better get back to it. We were about to move the body before he arrived and started shouting the odds. Another minute and he would have seen us hauling her body out of the car and onto the sheet."

"Another reason why a marquee is called for in these situations," Katy suggested.

"Too right. We didn't feel it necessary, what with the cordon being right back, away from the garages. I've changed my mind, I'll get them to erect one first and then get the body shifted."

"I think that would be wise. In my opinion, he was riled up enough to come back here for a second round."

"I hear you. What are you up to now that you've spoilt the parents' day?"

"Thanks for rubbing it in. We're on our way to see what the CCTV footage has to offer from last night's incident."

"You might want to check this area out as well, while you're at it."

Katy raised an eyebrow and said, "You reckon? I would never have thought about that if you hadn't prompted me, I'm so glad we dropped by to see you, Patti."

Patti scowled at Katy. "You know what they say, sarcasm is the lowest form of wit."

"Whatever." Katy grinned. "We'll drop back and see you if we have any news to share."

"I'll be here, getting on with business as usual."

Katy and Charlie walked around the corner to the security building. Standing outside were Jack and Eric, surveying the area around them.

"Everything all right, gents?" Katy asked.

Eric jumped and spun around to face her. "Nearly caused me a heart attack, sneaking up on me like that, Inspector."

"Sorry, I wasn't aware that I had. Is everything okay?" Katy repeated, doubts filling her mind at their worried expressions.

"Yes, yes, everything is hunky dory with us. We've been busy whiling away the time until you returned. We expected you back sooner."

"Sorry, it was our intention to return sooner than this,

but we were held up, explaining what happened to Tina's parents."

"Ah, yes," Jack said. "I won't bother asking how they took the news."

"As expected. Right, have you managed to find anything?"

"We haven't had the chance to whizz through it, we got called to sort out several jobs in your absence."

Katy doubted the truth behind his words, given that they were caught standing around twiddling their thumbs. "Are you free to take us through the discs now?"

"Oh yes, we're ready for you. Lead the way, Eric, this is more your domain than mine since the new system has been installed."

Eric smiled and shook his head. "You're an old dinosaur, that's your problem, Jack, you're stuck in your ways and hate any form of change."

"I'm not going to deny that. Lead on, boy, lead on."

The two men entered the building ahead of Katy and Charlie. The room where all the security monitors were housed was at the rear of the building, the door to which was closed and needed Eric to open it with the key draped around his neck.

"Come into our inner sanctum, ladies."

He threw back the door and stepped aside. Katy's mouth fell open at the vast area laid out with sophisticated security equipment from floor to ceiling. "Bloody hell. This is some place. No wonder you're struggling to get your head around it all, Jack. I think I would have problems, too."

"Thanks, try telling that to the dean. I'm not sure she believes me, thinks I'm pulling a fast one, she does. Has even told me to buck my ideas up. In other words, she's willing to replace me with a younger model or possibly expecting Eric here to cover the whole campus single-handedly."

"It's a piece of piss," Eric added.

He jumped into action, and Jack closed the door behind them and stood back to let his accomplished partner get the task done.

Katy glanced over her shoulder and smiled at Jack. "Don't get downhearted, Jack, I'm sure Eric will go through the intricacies of the new equipment, if you ask him to. Don't be too proud to admit you're struggling with getting to grips with things."

"Thanks for the rallying words, but I think my time in this game is almost up. Maybe the dean is right, she should be on the lookout for my replacement after all these years."

"How long have you been here?"

"Coming up to thirty years now, and yes, I know I don't look old enough."

He and Katy both laughed.

"Why don't you consider it this way? Change is inevitable with all the improvements in technology coming our way daily. Grasp the challenge with both hands, that's what I do."

"You have problems with technology, too, is that what you're telling me?"

"All the time. My partner is always getting me out of trouble. I'm never too proud to ask when I know something is beyond me, it's how we learn in life."

"Yeah, but at my time of life I think it's time I stopped learning. My brain wants to slow down like the rest of my body. No chance of that happening with all this newfangled stuff to learn, is there?"

"I suppose. Either you want to learn or you don't. Again, it depends on your age and capabilities to soak up information."

"Yeah, that's what's troubling me. The body is willing, the mind, not so much."

Katy rubbed the top of his arm. "Why don't we watch

what Eric is up to? You might learn a snippet or two to start you off."

"I doubt it. These youngsters don't do anything slow and steady these days, they're always flying around at mega warp speed. Observe the rate his fingers are inputting the information into that keyboard. I ain't no touch typist, I can barely use one finger well enough, let alone ten of them."

Katy's heart went out to the man who, listening to him, had given up on his career.

"What's that?" Charlie asked. She leaned over Eric's shoulder to get a better view.

"It's too dark to tell. Let me whizz over to the camera on the other side, see if we can obtain a better image. If not, we're buggered. Sorry, pardon my language, I shouldn't say that with ladies present."

"Quite right. What have I told you about controlling that foul mouth of yours whilst on duty?" Jack reprimanded him.

"Sorry, I apologise profusely," Eric mumbled.

"Don't, it's fine, we hear worse down at the nick, I can assure you," Charlie said.

"Right, this is the other angle. What's this here?" Eric zoomed in on a person lingering by the doorway to the building.

"Is he coming out or going in?" Katy asked. She was viewing the image on a screen above Eric's head.

He flicked a switch, and all ten monitors had the same view.

"Wow, I didn't know that was even possible," Jack said in awe.

Katy leaned in and whispered, "Neither did I to tell you the truth."

She laughed, and Jack grimaced and shrugged as if to say, 'I rest my case. It's time to throw in the towel once and for all'.

"Don't do anything rash. I'd be disappointed in you if you took that stance. Eric seems a nice enough lad, he'll give you some worthwhile tips, I'm sure, won't you, Eric?"

"What? Oh, yeah. You're not saying anything I haven't told Jack myself," Eric confirmed. "Here they are again. Let's slowly move it on, see if I can enhance the image a little with this button here."

The four of them watched in anticipation as Eric worked his magic.

"Yes, you're getting there." Charlie slapped him on the shoulder. "A bit more if you can."

"I can't, it has reached its limit now."

Katy tutted. "Maybe the lab can enhance it better at their end. Can you run us off a copy, Eric?"

"Sure thing. It won't take me a second." Eric pressed a few buttons and then handed Charlie a disc in a plastic case.

Katy couldn't be more impressed with the young man's speed and proficiency, and again, her heart went out to Jack when she saw his shoulders slump beside her. "Use it to your advantage. Don't see it as a negative, turn it into a positive," Katy whispered.

He shook his head and murmured, "I can't. I'm too old for this shit."

"I never took you as a defeatist, Jack."

"I'm not, normally."

The screen altered, and the garage area came into view. Again, the image was taken at night. The clock said one-forty. The garage door opened, and the lone figure slipped through the gap. The person remained inside for a further three minutes and then left the garage, pausing only to check the area was clear before they bolted.

"Can you track the person?" Katy asked.

"I can try. It might take me a few minutes to get everything I need to hand," Eric replied.

"We're not going anywhere anytime soon," Charlie told him. She peered over her shoulder at Katy.

Katy nodded. "That's right. We'd be foolish to move, if we have who we believe to be the perpetrator before us. Looks like we can put both deaths down as murder now."

"I thought as much," Eric said. "There's no way Tina would have killed herself, she was far too smart to do anything that stupid."

"How would you know?" Jack jumped in.

"We've had a few chats, that's all. Nothing more than that, Jack, I promise. She was a really nice girl. It's terrible that this person chose to take her out, if that's what has happened."

"Exactly. If this is all we have to go on, all this person is guilty of so far is coming out of an out-of-bounds building, as well as entering and leaving the garage early this morning," Katy recapped the evidence they had to hand.

"Is that going to be enough to throw at this person, if we ever catch up with them?" Charlie asked.

"We have enough to place them at both crime scenes, it's up to us to find more, with Eric's help. What do you say, Eric?"

"All I can do is try for you. It might take a while to sift through all the camera footage we have available on site."

"How many cameras are we talking about?" Katy asked.

"Around fifty, give or take a few that haven't been set up properly as yet. The installers are coming back to get them working in a few weeks."

"Wow, that's an impressive setup. Well, I'm hopeful you can come up trumps for us, Eric."

"I'll do it for Tina. She didn't deserve to die, neither of them did, even though they probably conned that key out of me."

"What key?" Jack was quick to pounce. "No, no, no, don't tell me you gave them the key to that building?"

Eric's head dropped. "Sorry, Jack. I know it was wrong but…"

"No buts. You're to blame for that girl losing her life, no one else," Jack retaliated.

Katy raised a hand. "Now, Jack, I think that's going way over the top. If Eric made a call that was wrong, he's going to have to deal with the consequences for the rest of his life."

"I feel gutted," Eric said, his voice catching in his throat. "They promised me they would behave, and up until last night, everything was fine."

"How long have they had the key, Eric?" Katy asked.

"I gave it to one of the lads a few weeks ago. He told me that Tina had requested it and that she was too shy to ask me herself."

"So your ego allowed this to happen," Jack shouted.

He pointed at Eric, and Katy noted his hand was shaking.

"Calm down, Jack," Katy warned. "What's done is done, there's little we can do about it now. At least we know how the students gained access to the building."

"It's all well and good telling me to calm down, you're not the one who got a verbal warning for allowing the students to have access to that building, *I did*."

"Shit!" Eric seethed. "I'm sorry, you should have told me. I'll put that right with Dean Johnson as soon as I've finished here."

"There you go, I knew Eric would offer to do the right thing," Katy said. She rested her hand on Jack's forearm.

He pulled it away. "The damage has already been done. She'll think I've persuaded him to take the fall for me, to save my own neck. Bugger, I've had it with all of this shit. I'm out of here. Explain that to the dean when you see her. I gave my all to this university over the years, and *he* comes along and puts a dent in my efforts within a few months. Nope, I'm done and dusted, there's no way back from this, not when I can't trust the person I'm working alongside. I've never had to deal with this kind of crap before and I have no intention of dealing with it this time either."

"Jack, please," Katy insisted, "take a second to mull things over before you take that leap into the unknown. Can you afford to pack it all in? The way the economy is at the moment? Don't cut your nose off, that would be my advice."

Eric left his seat and approached Jack. "Please, Jack, don't do it. I've told you I'll make amends. Give me the opportunity to put this right. I can't do this job without you, I just can't. We're buddies, partners in crime. We get on like father and son, or at least I thought we did. Don't tell me you've never slipped up in your younger days? I'm still learning the ropes. I'll be far more vigilant and less trusting of the students in the future, I swear I will."

Katy smiled. She thought Eric had pleaded his case well, and her gaze turned to Jack, imploring him not to walk out and to allow Eric to do the right thing and admit to his mistakes. Either way, she hoped they would get on with it. Time was money, and they were already against the clock on this one as it was. "You can't say fairer than that, Jack. Give Eric a chance, eh?"

Jack took a step towards the door and then retreated. He made the same move repeatedly until he let out a huge sigh. "Okay, I'm going to relent and give you one last chance, Eric. Don't let me down again, ever."

"I won't, I promise. Yay, okay, I'll get back to work now." Eric gleefully jumped back into his chair and hit his keyboard.

The screens took on a life of their own once more, reverting back to the images that were on them before Eric had concentrated on the two crime scene areas. Katy scanned all the images, tying to keep up with what he was doing. In the end, it proved too much for her, and she closed her eyes for fear of going cross-eyed.

Eventually, Eric managed to locate the lone figure leaving the campus at the north end. "There they go, heading off into town."

"Isn't the train station that way?" Charlie asked.

"It is. Maybe this person lives locally and isn't a resident student. If they were, the dorms are over the other side of the campus," Eric proposed.

"Or they could be pulling our chain, misleading us intentionally," Charlie suggested. "He or she might switch their appearance and show up on the other side later. Can you zoom in on the cameras by the dorms and run through them for me, Eric?"

He did. However, the outcome was disappointing.

In the end, Katy decided to leave it there for the day. They had a significant lead for a possible suspect and evidence that Forensics might be able to enhance to get the investigation underway.

"Before we drop these discs over to the lab, we need to have a quick chat with the lecturers."

"I bet that's going to prove to be a waste of time," Charlie grumbled.

CHAPTER 6

*A*fter interviewing the professors, which proved as Charlie had predicted, to be a waste of time, they dropped the discs off at the lab and returned to the station. Graham took one look at them and insisted he nip out to grab a sandwich for each of them before the baker's shut.

"You're an absolute star. I don't care what the others say about you behind your back, Graham, you'll do for me." Katy winked and accepted the offered sandwich he was holding out to her.

"Don't listen to the boss, Graham, I never do," Charlie said. She took the bag he offered her and peered inside.

"They only had cheese and tomato or ham and tomato. I took a punt on who would prefer which."

"Great, I've got the ham one," Katy said, less than enthusiastic at the curled-up offering.

Charlie groaned. "Don't tell me, you want to swap."

"You don't mind, do you?"

"Like I have an option." Charlie switched bags and sipped at her coffee.

Katy munched on a corner of her sandwich and then

addressed the team, informing them of how things had developed at the university that morning. "So, it would seem that we're on the lookout for an individual who is keen on keeping us guessing, judging by the shifty way he dresses and skulks around the place."

"Do you think the perp was aware of where the cameras on campus are, boss?" Graham asked. He placed his hands behind his head and tipped back in his chair.

"It would appear to be the case. The young security guard slipped up by allowing the students to gain access to the roof."

"Do you think the culprit is a member of the group, or are we saying that he's likely got it in for all of them?" Patrick asked.

"Hard to say at this point. Charlie and I have to compare notes on the rest of the group. My first inclination would be to say it's someone from outside the group; they seem to be a close-knit unit. Maybe another student is jealous of the way they get on so well together, but then, would another student have it in them to set up the two deaths as suicides to cover the fact that both girls were murdered? I find that hard to believe, not impossible by a long shot, but still considerably hard to believe."

"I agree," Charlie said. "Let's hope Forensics come up trumps with a possible ID of the suspect, because without that, we're screwed."

"That's true," Katy admitted reluctantly. "What about background checks, have those been carried out in our absence?" She directed the question at Karen Titchard.

"I've made a start on the people involved in the first case but I haven't got around to the second one yet. I don't usually ask for help, boss, but in this instance, I fear I'm going to need it."

"Your wish is my command. Stephen, why don't you lend Karen a hand on this one?"

Stephen left his desk and pulled up a chair next to Karen. "Do with me what you will, Karen, within reason."

Karen snorted and rolled her eyes. "In your dreams, Elliot."

Katy left them to it and scribbled down some extra notes on the whiteboard. Her phone rang in the office, and she dashed across the room to answer it. "DI Katy Foster, how can I help?"

"Are you busy?" Sean Roberts had a distinctive voice that Katy recognised as soon as she heard it.

"Not really, ooops, I should have replied, yes, always. Do you want to see me?"

"I'll get Trisha to make us both a coffee. See you soon."

"I'm on tenterhooks already," she responded and ended the call.

It was unusual for the chief to summon her. Yes, he dropped in or caught up with her occasionally in the hallway but rarely felt the need to request her company in his office. Her stomach flipped over several times during the walk from her office to his. Trisha greeted her with a friendly smile.

"Go straight through, Inspector. I'll bring your coffee in to you in a moment."

"Always a welcome experience, thanks, Trisha. Umm… what sort of mood is he in, or shouldn't I ask?"

"He's fine, quite chilled today, so he's not going to tear you off a strip, at least I don't think that's on the cards."

Katy blew out a relieved breath. "That's good."

"Go through," Trisha said a second time.

Maybe she could sense Katy's reluctance to enter the lion's den. She knocked on the door and entered the room after Sean bellowed for her to come in.

"Hello, sir. You wanted to see me?" She closed the door

behind her and crossed the room to his desk, studying him en route.

"Yes, don't look so worried, unless there's something you haven't told me and there should be a reason for concern."

"There's not. I'm just surprised to have received your call out of the blue. Is everything all right?"

"Fine. I wanted a quick update on the case I've heard you're dealing with on the grapevine. Care to fill me in?"

Trisha put a halt to the conversation when she entered the room and deposited the cups and saucers on the desk in front of them. "I've brought you a couple of biscuits, too, in case you haven't had time for lunch yet, Inspector. I know how busy you are."

"That's kind of you. As it happens, I had a dried-up sandwich a bit earlier. I think I threw half of it in the bin."

Trisha offered up a sympathetic smile and left the room. Katy picked up a custard cream and nibbled on it, resisting the temptation to dunk it in her coffee and laughed when Sean did exactly that.

"You can't have a biscuit and not dunk it, Inspector. Get in there, that's an order."

"Who am I to argue?" She did the same and savoured the biscuit soaked in coffee.

"So, tell me about your latest case, or should I say cases?"

Swilling down the biscuit with a couple of sips of coffee, Katy took the opportunity to prepare her speech. "Well, at first, it appeared that both victims succeeded in taking their own lives, but now we think differently."

He inclined his head whilst holding his large cup in both of his hands. "What makes you think that? Any evidence indicating that to be the case?"

"The first victim had small nicks on her throat. The pathologist believes she was possibly held at knife point and maybe forced to jump from the roof of a building."

"A public building?"

"No, we've since found out that the two victims belonged to a group of students who 'persuaded' one of the security guards on campus to give them a key, allowing them access to the roof."

"For what purpose? And at this time of year?"

"Exactly. The other members of the group have assured us there was no malicious intent involved, they merely went up there after lectures to be with one another and to chill out."

Sean raised an eyebrow and took another sip from his cup. "Too much time on their hands?"

"Possibly. The first victim, Paula Lowe, was married. I would have thought she would have better things to do than hang around with a bunch of hormonal teenagers but what do I know?"

"I would say the same. Okay, moving on, tell me what you've found out about the second victim."

"Not very much as yet. We stumbled across the young woman when the security guard found her in a garage. The car was running. I'm assuming she died of carbon monoxide poisoning."

"Bloody hell not something we hear a lot about, is it? Teens going out that way."

"I know. It's puzzling."

"You said the security guard found her, the same guard who gave the group access to the building?"

"That's correct."

"Have you questioned him about this?"

"I have," she lied. "I've decided to put it down to pure coincidence, sir."

"Hmm... not sure I would have done the same. Never mind, you're the one running this case, not me."

Katy smiled and knocked back another couple of mouthfuls of coffee. "I can't really tell you much more about the second case because the pathologist couldn't share many details with me at the scene. I'm awaiting the PM report, which should be back within the next day or two."

"You're obviously linking both crimes, I take it?"

"Hard to dismiss it. The girls were good friends, and now they're both dead. We analysed the CCTV footage the security guard—yes, the same one—found in the system. We picked up a lone figure, dressed in the usual dark clothing outside the building and the garage around the time of the deaths."

Sean sat upright. "So you do have a suspect on your radar then?"

"Yes, but that's as far as it goes for now. We've dropped the footage over at the lab on the way back to the station. They're going to see if they can enhance the images, which will hopefully lead us to the culprit."

"And if it doesn't?"

"Then we'll have to solve the investigation the old-fashioned way. We've done it before and no doubt we'll have to do it again in the future. The team are carrying out the usual background checks now on the families. Nothing has shown up with the husband or the parents of Paula Lowe so far."

"I don't envy you. Is there anything I can do to help?"

"I don't think so, not at this point. It's still early days. We're hoping something will break for us soon, but that's not likely, given what we've come across already."

"What was this married woman doing hanging around with a group of teenagers?"

Katy shrugged. "She chucked in her job and decided she wanted to enrol in a psychology course at uni. By all accounts, she met the rest of the group during lectures and bonded with them. Nothing untoward there, not unless I'm missing something obvious."

"Might be worth digging more into that side of things. Has the group had any hassle from anyone else on campus? Is there such a thing as gang rivalry on a university campus? I'm well out of my depth there."

"Again, I don't think so. I'll run it past Dean Johnson, she's really cut up about all this happening on her watch. I did loosely question her before the second incident cropped up, and she didn't have a clue what was going on."

"No other incidents of this nature ever happened on site before?"

"No, she's been there a while, that's why she was upset because they have an exemplary record to date. They have counsellors in place. She mentioned it was touch and go during the pandemic but no one had ever committed suicide on site before."

"But they weren't suicides, we're talking murder, Katy," he reminded her.

"I'm aware of that, sir, but at the time of questioning the dean, we didn't really know what we were dealing with."

"I'm with you. So what's your next move?"

"We need to see what Forensics come up with and go from there. Our hands are well and truly tied. Yes, we'll continue to do the background checks and investigate every minor detail we pick up, but apart from that…"

"Okay, well, I'm here if you need to run anything past me, or if you need me to pull in any favours for you during the investigation, just shout."

"Thanks, sir, I really appreciate it."

"How are things in general? At home? Is AJ enjoying his new job?"

"It's okay. His business is going from strength to strength, so much so that he's employed a young lady to be his assistant."

"A young lady, eh?" Sean teased. "And you're okay with that?"

Katy shrugged. "I've got to be. I trust him." Even to her ears there was a note of doubt to her words.

Sean cocked an eyebrow, and a glimmer of a smile surfaced. "Not sure who you're trying to convince with that one, Inspector. Adding a note of caution here, if you'll allow me to. AJ loves you, he would never cheat on you. Take it from me, he's not the type. You have the perfect setup, him being at home looking after Georgie while you work."

Katy wagged her pointed finger. "Not any more. He's busier than normal now. All right, he works around our daughter's school hours, but there is going to come a time when the business is going to explode. It's that what's concerning me, I suppose."

"Have you voiced your concerns with AJ?"

"Not really, no."

"If I learnt one thing when my marriage crumbled, it was that I stopped caring. Don't walk in my shoes. Don't let things disintegrate before your eyes. I realise how difficult it is keeping your eye on the ball all the time at work and at home, but you're a smart lady, you can do it with your hands tied whilst being blindfolded."

"I'm glad you have that much faith in me, sir."

"I have. I've never seen anything in you to tell me otherwise. Now get out of here and go find yourself a killer to hunt down. It'll help vent any pent-up feelings you might have stirring up your insides."

"With respect, sir, you come out with the weirdest sayings at times."

"Yeah, I think your predecessor used to tell me the same. Talking of which, have you heard from Lorne lately?"

"Last I heard she was back at work with the Norfolk Constabulary and loving life again."

He smiled. "I think we both expected that, didn't we? You can't keep a good police officer down, ever."

"Yeah, so the old saying goes. It's definitely true in her case."

"Don't I know it? She's like the proverbial boomerang, always coming back to the Force. Good luck to her, I wish there were more officers of her calibre returning to the Force these days. Sadly, that's not the case."

"The Met in particular has gone through a tough time recently, sir."

"It has. I've done my very best to stamp out the behaviour highlighted in certain cases and through the press in the past few years, but it's a daunting and thankless task. Let me ask you this: have you ever had a problem with the way I've dealt with you over the years?"

"Speaking as a female officer?"

"Yes."

"No, never. For a start, I would never have put up with it. Talking of my predecessor, neither would she."

"Glad you think that. If that should change in the future, feel free to slap me down at any time, won't you?"

"I will. Especially now that you've given me permission to do so. I must get on. Thanks for the chat, sir."

"Keep me posted with how things progress, and don't forget, I'm here if you need a hand."

She rose from her seat, headed towards the door and threw over her shoulder, "Champing at the bit to get out in the field again, sir?"

"You know me far too well, Inspector."

During the return journey, Katy mulled over his words of wisdom regarding her marriage. She had a lot of sorting out to do when she got home that evening.

CHAPTER 7

*K*aty drove into work feeling more at peace with herself than she had done in months. The previous evening, after getting home at a reasonable hour, she had bathed Georgie with AJ and put her to bed then shared a romantic meal with her husband over a bottle of wine.

They had held an open discussion about their marriage for the first time in years, each of them voicing their concerns of where they believed they had gone off the track and how to put their relationship back on an even keel once more. AJ had gone to great lengths, even breaking down in tears at one point, to assure her that he would never stray and that he loved her more and more each and every day. It was the reassurance she needed to put their recent spat behind them.

She and AJ had always been the strongest couple she had known, that was aside from her former partner, Lorne and her husband, Tony.

Katy arrived at work to find a strange car in her allocated spot. Charlie was sitting in the passenger seat. She waved and held a finger up then leaned over and gave the driver a kiss on the lips. *Hmm... must be her new fella.* She drummed her fingers on the steering wheel and waited for Charlie's young man to reverse out of her space. Which he did not long after, then he put his foot down and sped out of the car park and onto the main road. Katy drew into her space and met up with a red-faced Charlie at the main entrance.

"Was that your new young man?"

"It was. Sorry, he followed me into work and plonked himself in your slot before I had the chance to warn him not to."

"It's fine. You might want to advise him to tone it down a bit with that fast car of his, especially outside the cop shop."

"Yeah, I cringed when he floored the accelerator. I'll have a word in his ear."

"You do that, otherwise he's going to alert every uniformed copper to be on the lookout for him in the future."

Charlie cringed. "Yeah, silly man, eh?"

"Indeed. I'm presuming he stayed over last night."

Katy pushed open the door and stepped inside. Charlie didn't respond until they had passed through the security door and were ascending the concrete stairs up to the first floor. "You might be right."

"Go easy, Charlie. Watch you're not on the rebound from Brandon."

"I will, I promise. He's so cute, he has me wrapped around his little finger already."

Katy sighed inwardly. That much was clear by what she'd seen of the little toerag already. She knew it wasn't right to judge someone upon first meeting them, but she had a nose for spotting the wrong type and was surprised at Charlie, falling for someone who was so blatantly wrong for her. Maybe she was guilty of going over the top with her character assassination, but this was her partner she was dealing with here. Someone she had known for years, mostly through working alongside her mother, so she was keen to throw a protective arm around Charlie's shoulders if the wrong person infiltrated her life.

Katy decided to ignore the comment and entered the incident room to find the rest of the team all hard at it. "Morning, all. Please note the tinge of colour in my partner's cheeks."

Every eye turned Charlie's way. "Gee, thanks for making me blush even more, boss."

"I'll leave it there. Any news from anyone yet? If not, why not? We need to get this investigation moving, quick smart." When no one responded, Katy marched ahead and into her office, frustration already gnawing at her bones. Ignoring the daily grind of opening the mail and tending to her emails, she opted instead to ring Patti first thing.

"Yes," Patti replied warily.

"Umm... I was hoping you might have some news for me regarding Tina Webster's PM, if you've managed to do it yet."

"Oh, you were, were you? Well, as it happens, I was in the middle of typing up my report now."

"How exciting, or is it?"

"Depends how you look at it."

"Sounds ominous. Just give me the gist of it in a nutshell, if you don't mind."

"She was murdered."

"Wow, okay, I wasn't expecting you to be so blunt. How can you tell?"

"There was swelling on her face. I believe the perpetrator hit her, knocking her unconscious, and then set the scene up for us to think she had committed suicide."

"The brick on the accelerator?"

"Correct."

"I had a feeling that would be the case. Shit. I'll need to get in touch with her parents to let them know, unless you've already done it."

"No chance. Not after the confrontation I had with Mr Webster at the scene yesterday."

Katy chuckled. "I thought as much. Bugger, two murders in as many days, and nothing as such to go on. I don't suppose you know how long the Forensics team are going to be with the footage?"

"Nope, that's your department to keep on top of them."

"Is it? Since when?"

"Since I've been too busy dealing with your PM for you."

"Okay, I'll chase them up now. Can you put me through?"

"Bloody hell. I might as well give them a bell myself. I'll call you back."

Katy hung up, wearing a huge grin after another successful ploy had been deposited.

True to her word, Patti called back a few minutes later. "Bad news for you."

"Bugger, can't they do it?"

"It doesn't look likely. They believe the image is as good as it's going to get."

"That figures. You should have seen the equipment on show at the university, we're talking state-of-the-art kind of stuff. Shit! It doesn't solve our problem, though, does it?"

"Nope. Can I get on now? Or do you need to vent some more?"

"Now you've asked…"

Patti let out a large guttural groan.

Katy tried really hard to hold back the laughter but failed.

Patti cursed a few expletives and slammed the phone down, leaving Katy to tackle her morning post whilst chuckling now and then. She was a third of the way through the mind-numbing task, flicking from brown envelope to answering the odd email here and there, when Charlie came flying into the room. "What's wrong?"

"We need to go out. A young man's body has been found on a railway track."

Katy slotted her arms into her jacket, which was warming the back of her chair, and followed Charlie out of the room. It wasn't until they were halfway down the stairs that Katy asked, "Where?"

"I thought you'd never ask. Just around the corner from the university, otherwise I would have left it for uniform and the pathologist to sort out."

"You're getting a sixth sense for this. Don't ever tell me you're going to ensure you do your policing via the proper channels, unlike your mother."

"How did I know you were going to sling that one at me?"

"Must be that gut instinct kicking in again. Once it starts, there's no stopping it. It's like a runaway train."

Charlie tutted. "Get out of here. It won't work."

"What won't?" By now they had reached the bottom of the stairs, and Katy pushed through the door that led into the reception area.

"You trying to pull the wool over my eyes."

Katy slapped a hand over her chest, and her eyes widened. "Shame on you for thinking such a thing."

Charlie chose to keep quiet.

They passed by the desk sergeant. "We're on our way out to the scene. Is it a bloody one?"

"I don't think it's too bad, ma'am," Mick said.

"Bad enough that a young man has lost his life, though, eh?"

Mick scratched the side of his head. "Yes, sorry. What was I thinking?"

"No idea. We'll be there soon. I hope your team is doing the necessary to keep prying eyes from nosing around."

"It's all in hand down there. I sent two more teams to ensure things run smoothly, ma'am."

"Glad to hear it, Mick. See you later."

THE AREA WAS SWAMPED with uniformed officers. At least six of them were trying to keep the crowd back behind the cordons that had been put in place. Over to the right, Katy noticed a white van pulling up and a couple of members of the local SOCO team getting out and going to the back of the van. She headed their way after realising she hadn't replenished the stock of suits she had used recently.

"Hi, guys, any chance we can nick a few suits off you."

"Sure, what size? No, don't bother answering, we're getting a bit short ourselves and only have large ones available."

"They'll likely drown us, but that's better than nothing. Thanks. Daft question, but has Patti been informed?"

"Yes, she's right behind us. Told us to come on ahead while she finished up a PM report. One of yours by any chance?"

"Possibly. All right if we accompany you to the scene?" Katy asked.

"Why not? We'll trundle over there once we've gathered our equipment. Won't be a tick."

Katy and Charlie slipped on the oversized suits and giggled at each other.

"Christ, I don't think we'll be winning any awards on the catwalks wearing these monstrosities," Katy quipped.

"I was about to suggest the same. The white is fetching enough, but the shape leaves a lot to be desired."

"If you're ready, ladies?" Rick, the head tech, asked.

"Lead the way," Katy told him.

He did just that. They sauntered alongside the track for

about a hundred yards until they came to a mound that had been hidden by a clean dust sheet, Katy suspected by a caring uniformed copper. A female officer was standing off to the side, and she and Katy exchanged knowing glances before Katy nodded at her.

"Let's see what we have here then," Rick said. "I've instructed the rest of the team to get the marquee up as quickly as possible." He jerked his head at the crowd straining their necks on the platform close by.

"Good idea. No one should see this."

Rick pulled the sheet off the body, and Katy stared at the figure down at her feet.

"Fuck! We know him."

Charlie nudged her arm. "We do. Who is it?"

"Tyler Dodds. What the fuck is going on here, Charlie? That's three members of the group now dead within a few days of each other."

"Are we looking at another murder that has been made out to be a suicide?" Charlie asked.

Rick crouched beside the body and blew out a breath. "Apparently, the train was unable to stop. It was dark, and the driver didn't see the body on the track until it was too late."

Katy's gaze ran the length and breadth of the young man's body. She found it incredibly hard to believe what she was seeing. This type of thing was unheard of. Both of his thighs had been crushed along with one of his arms, which had all been tied to the track. The other arm was lying across his chest.

"I guess we can rule out suicide this time round," Charlie said.

"You reckon?"

Charlie cringed. "Sorry for stating the obvious, my bad."

"You're all right. Jesus, now we have another horrendous

task on our hands, informing his parents. Why is this happening? Why them?"

"Umm... I think my priority would be to gather the rest of the group together and to try and keep them safe," Charlie muttered beside her.

"Of course, we're going to need to do that, it goes without saying," Katy snapped uncharacteristically. She took a moment and then looked at Charlie. "Sorry, that was uncalled for. I'm going to give the chief a call. He said he wanted to be more involved in this investigation, well, he can dig around, searching for a safe house we can use."

"Will the other parents be up for that?"

"Tough if they have any objections. I don't see what else we can bloody do. While I'm calling the chief, I think you should ring Dean Johnson, she'll need to be informed. Ask her to request the rest of the group to join her in one of the classrooms, and tell her we'll be down there shortly, after we've spoken to Patti." Another van arrived and pulled up alongside the SOCO vehicle. "Talk of the Devil and she will appear."

Charlie chuckled. "Don't for Christ's sake let her hear you say that."

"Don't worry, I'm not that stupid, I know how touchy she can be. Let's get this show on the road."

Charlie drifted off and made her call while Katy remained close to the body and rang Sean Roberts.

"Katy, is everything okay?" Roberts asked, his concern evident in his tone.

"I'm okay, but everything isn't fine and dandy here. I'm out in the field. Actually, I'm standing next to a train track not far from the university and..."

"Damn, you're attending another murder scene, am I right?"

"Spot on. A member of the same group has been tied to

the tracks, and unfortunately, the driver didn't see him, and you can fill in the blanks. I'm presuming that he was killed outright."

"Heck. What do you need from me?"

"I hate to ask but I think the time for discussion has now passed and action needs to take place right away."

"All right. In the form of what?"

"You asked me to reach out if I needed assistance with anything. I do. I need to sort out a safe house for the rest of the kids. I think it's imperative that we try to keep them together, out of harm's way until we arrest the perpetrator."

"I wholeheartedly agree. I'll see if I can pull some strings and get a house for you by the end of the day."

"If not sooner would be preferable, boss."

"Leave it with me."

He ended the call, and Katy peered over her shoulder to see Charlie coming towards her.

"How did she take the news?" Katy waved her hand, dismissing her own question. "No, don't bother answering such a dumb question."

"I wasn't going to," Charlie replied. "The dean is going to ensure the students are safe. She's even going to ask Jack and Eric to guard them until she hears back from us. I told her that you were trying to source a safe house."

"That's great news. I think it allows us to at least take a breather, for now. Here's Patti, let's see what she has to say about all of this."

"Did I hear my name mentioned?" Patti asked. She joined them and with her head shaking, she mumbled, "An utter waste of yet another young life."

"Agreed, and here's the thing, he was part of the same group."

"Sod it! That's terrible. What are you doing about that, Inspector?"

Katy raised an eyebrow and replied, "My best, just what you'd expect, Patti."

"Are you, though? Three young lives in three short days, how is that you doing your best?"

"Bloody charming! I expected better than that from you, Patti. I am, we are, as a team doing our damned best. I've even roped in the chief to help us today."

"Good. This investigation needs to be taken seriously if you have this many murders to deal with."

Katy frowned, and her suit rustled as she folded her arms. "What are you suggesting here?"

"Nothing, I'm just saying we need to get on top of the case, pronto, if you want to catch the perp in time. He's bound to go after the rest of the group."

"Stop right there, you're encroaching on my territory, Patti. All I need from you is to send me the PM reports in a timely fashion so that I can conduct my investigation properly. As you're well aware, I rang you barely an hour ago chasing up such reports and also seeing if anything had come back from the CCTV footage. Tell me I'm wrong." Katy's voice peaked at being just below high-pitched.

"All right, you don't have to take that tone with me, Inspector."

"Don't I? You've virtually stood there and accused me of slacking on this investigation. Without any frigging evidence to go on, how am I supposed to arrest the perpetrator? Give me a sodding break now and again, Patti, for fuck's sake."

"I'm sorry. That wasn't my intention. I think we're at crossed wires here. I wasn't telling you what you should be doing, more offering some sound advice."

Katy noted how sheepish Patti looked compared to when she had arrived and climbed down off her high horse. It was never a good idea to fall out with the pathologist during an investigation. "Okay, let's leave things there then. I always do my best with the information which is forthcoming from your department."

"I know. I've apologised, can we move on?" Patti said, her eyes drawn to the victim close to her feet.

"I wish we would. That's all I'm trying to do here, Patti, work the cases attached to this puzzling investigation. It's not easy with little, to no, evidence to go on."

"I appreciate that. Maybe the killer will have been sloppy here, if they knew the train was coming and were up against it, that's when slip-ups are likely made, aren't they?"

"True enough. Can you give me your expert opinion on this one? Only we'll need to leave soon, we've got the rest of the group to question and to keep safe."

"Ah, I might have known that you would have everything in hand."

"It is."

The pair of them crouched next to the body, their suits swishing with the movement and in the breeze that had got up.

"You're right, there's no doubt that he's been murdered, he couldn't have tied himself to the track."

"Do you think that's why one hand was left loose? The killer wanting us to believe he'd tied the rest of his limbs to the track?"

"More than likely. He would have been unable to do that double knot he has around his left wrist single-handedly."

"In other words, the killer slipped up," Katy filled in the gap.

"Indeed. We'll get the rope tested for prints, he might have slipped up there also."

"Sounds good to me. Anything else?"

"We'll check his clothes and body for any stray hairs et cetera. I have a good feeling about this one now, Katy."

Katy stared at the body of the young man who'd once had

an endearing nature and sighed. "None of these kids deserved to end up in a mortuary fridge. I'm determined to get to the bottom of this, but I can't if we haven't got the evidence to back up our theories, Patti. Go the extra mile for us and do your best to come up with the results we need to find this vile taker of lives."

"You have my word. Now shoo, if you have no further questions. I think it's imperative that we get him shifted off the tracks and back to the mortuary, allowing the rail service to get back on track for the day."

"Ouch, did you really just say that?"

Patti winced. "I'm afraid it popped out, you're going to have to forgive me."

"This time I will. Okay, I'll be in touch later if I find out anything from the other students. Sorry for being so touchy."

"Me, too. I think we were as bad as each other."

"I'll accept that. Friends? I hate being enemies. We'll check in with you later. I must fly now."

"Go. I don't want to hold you up."

Katy and Charlie disrobed and threw their suits and shoe covers into the black sack close to the cordon and jumped into the car and headed for the university. Katy drew into a spot close to the main entrance and flopped forward, resting her head on the steering wheel.

Charlie put a hand on her forearm and asked, "Is everything all right, Katy?"

"Yes, I need to take a breather, that's all, before I reveal another death to the rest of the group. I'm trying to put myself in their shoes. To grieve at their age over losing one friend is bad enough, but now three of them have been murdered, shit, they're going to be distraught, I just know it."

"We can't think like that. All we can do is our jobs and not think of the consequences. Are you struggling to hold it together?"

"No, not really struggling. I suppose I'm more conscious of what's going on around me at the moment and it's hard dealing with it. These kids had their whole lives ahead of them, and here we are, about to break the news to the same group of friends, who only yesterday were distressed beyond words."

"I know, life's so unfair, we're all aware of that. Let's deal with this first, then we'll have to drive over to the parents and tell them, or had you forgotten that part?"

"Pushed it aside rather than forgotten all about it," Katy admitted with a heavy heart. "Let's do this."

Dean Johnson was standing at the main entrance, one second rubbing her hands together and the next running them up and down her arms, trying to keep warm. "Ah, there you are. I have some bad news."

Katy's stomach rolled over. "Which is?"

"We can't find two of the students. Boris and Heidi. The others haven't seen them today at all. What in God's name is going on here? I was mortified to learn that Tyler had lost his life, such a nice young man, and now two more of the group have gone missing. How is that even possible?"

"Are the others being guarded now?" Katy motioned for them to make a move, and the dean jumped into action.

She led them down the long corridor towards her office. She stopped at a room they hadn't seen before and cast a sneaky glance over her shoulder. "It was either in here or I even considered putting the students over in the security building, but getting them there might have been too danger-ous, so I plumped for this option instead."

"I think you did the right thing."

The door opened to reveal Danny and Lizzie. They were sitting next to each other, their hands firmly held together. The second she laid eyes on Katy, Lizzie started crying.

Danny hooked an awkward arm around her shoulders and pulled her towards him. "It's all right. Hush now, Lizzie."

She pulled away from him and shouted, "Things will never be all right again. Now Boris and Heidi are both missing. What the fuck is going on? I'm petrified. I want to go home. I want my father."

Katy and Charlie both pulled up a chair at the desk closest to the two teenagers.

"We can't let you go home, Lizzie. We're making arrangements for you both to go to a safe house." Katy hoped she wasn't talking out of her arse and that Sean Roberts would have some news for her on that front soon.

"What? Just us? Not our families? Or do you mean our families as well?"

"No, we can't possibly house all of you. We believe the imminent threat lies with the members of the group, not your relatives. No one else's relatives have been harmed to date, have they?"

"I suppose so." Lizzie sniffled and wiped her nose on a fresh tissue she removed from a packet on the desk.

"Until we get the all-clear on that, we're going to need you to stick together, here." Katy shot a glance in the security guards' direction. "Jack and Eric will be watching over you. We'll ask Dean Johnson not to allow anyone to pass through the hallway outside. Do you understand me?"

"Yes." Lizzie nodded and started crying again. "But I'm scared. Is someone killing off our friends? Do you know who this person is? Or why they're doing it?"

"They're all valid questions that we simply don't have the answers to at this time, Lizzie. Hence us going to the extraordinary lengths, to ensure that you're both safe, and Heidi and Boris, once we track them down. I have to ask, do you know where either of them is?"

The pair shook their heads, and Danny picked up his phone that was lying on the desk.

"I've rung both of them dozens of times, left several messages on both phones and not had a single reply yet. Do you think something bad has happened to them? Like... Tyler?"

"At this stage, all we're trying to do is remain positive. I will issue an alert for Boris and Heidi. Can you give me their mobile numbers? We'll keep trying their phones and maybe we'll be able to trace them."

"Yes, you can trace their phones, that's an excellent idea, why didn't I think of that?" Danny said, his enthusiasm breaking out. "Can we ask how Tyler died, or would that be inappropriate at this time?"

"I can tell you roughly without going into too much detail. He was found up on the railway track, up the road."

"Did a train go over him?" Danny asked. "He usually caught the train home every night, his parents insisted it was the safest form of transport."

Katy nodded. "That's all you're going to get out of me for now. I don't want you to concern yourself with any of the deaths that have occurred in the last few days, I want you to think of the future. You're safe now, we're not going to let you out of our sight, I promise. What I'm going to need is your home addresses. I'll pop round and let your parents know what's going on."

"They're going to be livid," Lizzie said.

"Yeah, they are," Danny concurred. "Wouldn't you be if your child was whisked away to a safe house? I presume they're not going to be able to make contact with us during our stay, are they?"

"No. It would be for the best if there was zero contact between you and your parents."

"And we've got to stay here? Locked away, not seeing

anyone and worrying about our friends?" Lizzie complained, tears bulging in her pale-green eyes. "I can't believe it has come to this. First Paula dying, then Tina and Tyler, and now Boris and Heidi are missing as well. Can anyone tell us where this is going to end? Are we all going to die? To get killed by this shithead?"

Katy heaved out a reluctant sigh. "I'm sorry, I don't have all the answers or even some of the answers, not yet. All I have is a possible solution to keep you both safe, and Boris and Heidi, if we ever find them."

"It's a shame you didn't come to this conclusion yesterday, when Tyler was alive," Danny murmured.

"You have every right to think that way, Danny. All I can do is apologise but I know that won't bring Tyler back. I feel bad for letting him down, he was a lovely young man."

"He was great, they all were. It's driving me insane, trying to fathom out why someone would go out of their way to kill all three of them. Even when the truth eventually comes out, I will never understand why some bastard feels the need to take someone else's life. Who gives them the right to do that?"

"As I said, I don't have the answers to that particular question right now. Hopefully, something will come to light soon that will lead us to the killer's door. You have my word that my team and I will be working hard to ensure that happens. I feel it's only a matter of time now."

"I'm glad you're so confident. I spent most of last night going over the events of the last few days and came up blank. I can't think of one instance that could have sparked all of this hatred off, not one."

"At least you're trying to come up with a reason. Keep doing that for me. Ring me if anything comes to mind and you believe it is something we can act upon."

"I will. Lizzie and I will put our heads together, see what

we can think of. Umm... can I ask where this safe house is likely to be?"

"I'm not sure yet, probably somewhere fairly close by. You're not worried, are you?"

"No, not about being locked away somewhere for our own safety, it's what happens in between that is bugging me. What if the killer manages to get to either Lizzie or me? What if one of us needs to go to the toilet unaccompanied?"

"We won't be able to allow that. Either Jack or Eric will need to accompany you or Lizzie, just to be on the safe side."

Lizzie sniffled, drawing attention to herself. "It's all such a bloody mess. Who would have thought we'd be dealing with all this shit, this time last week?"

"She's right," Danny added. "It's totally unthinkable to both of us."

Katy smiled at them. "Which is why we need to ensure you're both safe for the interim. Hopefully you will only be inconvenienced for a few days, but if we didn't put you somewhere and something bad happened to one or both of you, I would never be able to forgive myself."

Lizzie and Danny clutched hands.

"We get that," Danny replied. "Where do you think Boris and Heidi are?"

"I really can't tell you that, not until I've spoken to their parents. Maybe they went off together somewhere. There's no chance they could be an item, is there?"

"No, not a chance in hell. Heidi is gay."

"Ah, okay. I don't suppose, as a group, you have access to another out-of-the-way area somewhere, do you?"

"No, the roof was the only place we chose to meet up, apart from the pub."

"Okay. Is there anything else you can tell me about either of them that you think should concern us?"

Lizzie and Danny held each other's gaze for a moment or two.

"No, I can't think of anything," Lizzie said. "Can you, Danny?"

"Something is there, at the back of my mind, but I don't know what."

Katy slid a business card in his direction. "If you recall what it is, contact me straight away."

"I will." Danny tucked the card into his jacket pocket.

Katy smiled again at the two students. "I have to go now, you'll be safe here. I don't want you to fret, okay?"

"We'll do our best, but it's not going to be easy," Lizzie admitted. "How long will it be before we hear about the house?"

"It shouldn't be too long. I'll keep chasing it, in between visiting Tyler's parents and yours. I won't let my boss sit on his backside doing nothing, I assure you." She tried to add a little humour to her response, hoping it would put Lizzie and Danny at ease.

The second she rose from her seat, Dean Johnson stepped forward to speak with her. "Are you leaving us now?"

"Yes." Katy gestured that they should step away from the students to continue their discussion.

"I don't mind telling you, I feel lost, unsure how to proceed. I want to remain here with Danny and Lizzie, to show them my support, but I have a busy schedule ahead of me today."

"Don't let this situation get on top of you, Fiona. I have every confidence that Jack and Eric have got the students' safety covered."

"Oh, I didn't mean to suggest otherwise. Anyway, I'll be just across the corridor if anything untoward should happen. I'm hoping against hope that isn't the case. Maybe I should cancel all my meetings today instead and stay here."

Katy shrugged. "That call has to be yours to make, no one else's. I think it would be wiser for you to get on with your day, keep to your normal schedule rather than add another unnecessary burden to your shoulders."

Fiona sighed, and her shoulders slumped. "I suppose you're right. Keep everything as it should be without any other major upheavals to contend with."

Katy placed a comforting hand on Fiona's forearm. "I think it's for the best. There's nothing stopping you from ringing Jack after every meeting, if only to put your mind at ease."

"That's a far more suitable suggestion to entertain. Thank you, Inspector."

She left the room with Katy and Charlie, only pausing for a brief moment or two to check if Jack had everything covered.

"Don't worry, Dean Jackson, between us, Eric and I have this. We'll put our lives on the line to protect those young 'uns, if necessary, won't we, Eric?"

"We will," Eric confirmed.

In the hallway, Katy and Charlie offered yet further assurances that Danny and Lizzie would be safe and left the building.

"She's a wreck," Charlie mumbled on the way back to the car.

"I think I would be, too, wouldn't you? She's doing her best to hold it together, which is a tough task for anyone faced with such adversities. Let's cut her some slack, shall we?"

CHAPTER 8

Tyler's mother was leaving her house when they arrived.

"Mrs Dodds. We'd like a quick chat with you before you go."

"I'm in a hurry, I have a hospital appointment that I can't be late for. What's this all about? Who are you?"

Katy held up her warrant card in front of the woman who was in her late forties.

She tugged her puffer jacket tighter around her body and folded her arms. "The police? What's this about? Oh, no, I think I can guess. Tyler mentioned that you'd been sniffing around down at the uni."

"Yes, it's to do with the investigation. We shouldn't keep you too long. Is there any chance we can have a chat inside?"

"In the car, or are you hinting at coming into the house?"

"The house would be preferable. Is Mr Dodds around?"

"No, he's out on the road, he's a long-distance haulage driver. Why? What do you need to see him for? 'Ere, you're worrying me now."

"I didn't mean to, please forgive me. Is your husband likely to be home soon?"

"Not for a few days, why? Get on with it, what's this all about?" Her eyes narrowed and pierced Katy's soul.

"Inside the house, if you don't mind, Mrs Dodds."

She huffed out a breath and hitched her bag onto her shoulder and returned to the house, shouting back, "This is against my better judgement, I'll have you know. You can take the flak from the consultant. I've waited nearly a year for this appointment, and now you two are going to mess it up for me. And yes, I'm livid in case you hadn't noticed."

"I'm sorry. There's simply no way around this issue." Katy skirted around the truth rather than blurt it out in the street, where her neighbours could hear. She could tell it was a roughish area, not wishing to cast unnecessary aspersions.

Mrs Dodds let them in and stood against the wall by the stairs, her arms folded once more. "Well, get on with it."

Katy swallowed down the bile burning her throat. "Mrs Dodds, it is with regret that we're here to tell you that your son, Tyler, lost his life today."

Mrs Dodds stared at Katy for a few awkward moments before her legs suddenly gave way beneath her and she ended up in a heap on the worn, discoloured pink carpet. "No," she screeched.

Katy took a step towards her, but the woman held up her hand.

"Don't come near me. How? Was it an accident? Or something worse... is it to do with what's happened to the other kids? Is it? What aren't you telling me? Come on, I want to hear everything."

"Shall we take a seat in the lounge? Maybe you'll be more comfortable there."

"Here's fine. Just tell me," she shrieked, her face turning crimson.

"Tyler was found tied to the railway track, close to the university."

"Bloody hell. So he was... murdered, like the others?"

"So it would appear, yes. I'm so sorry for your loss. I had to interview your son yesterday in connection with the investigation we're running, and he came across as a lovely young man."

"Who's now dead," his mother sneered. "Why? You lot should have been protecting him. I raised the subject with Tyler, and he assured me that he could look after himself. Clearly, he couldn't, otherwise he would still be with us now." She broke down in tears and crumpled to the floor. Then she thumped her clenched fists against her thighs. "Why? Why my baby? Why did it have to be him?"

Katy and Charlie glanced at each other, and Charlie shook her head.

Katy gulped down the saliva filling her mouth and took a step forward. "Please, Mrs Dodds, is there anyone we can call to come and be with you?"

"Yes, my sister, Jill." She jumped to her feet and fetched her handbag from the bannister where she had hooked it over the minute they had entered the house. Hands shaking, she fiddled with the catch and removed her mobile. She scrolled through her list of calls and tapped the screen. "Jilly, I need you to come to the house... yes, now. Don't ask... Jesus, woman, I said don't ask... all right, it's Tyler, he's gone." Mrs Dodds covered her eyes with her hand and cried. She held out the phone for Katy to take.

"Hello, Jill. I'm sorry, your sister is very upset. Is there any chance you can come and sit with her?"

"Who are you? She told me Tyler's gone. Has he run off somewhere?"

"I'm DI Katy Foster. Sadly, your nephew passed away this morning. We've had to break the news to his mother, your sister." Katy kicked herself for getting a little tongue-tied and stating the obvious.

"What the...? I'll be right there. Christ on a pogo stick, poor Tyler." The call ended.

"She's on her way. Are you all right?" Katy handed the phone back to Mrs Dodds whose glare intensified.

"Do you always ask such dumb questions at a time like this?"

Katy shrugged. "It has been known. It's never easy breaking such sad news to the victim's family."

"I would never have guessed. I need a drink." Mrs Dodds headed up the hallway.

"I can do that for you. You go and take a seat in the lounge, and I'll bring it in."

The woman stopped, turned and raced back to place her forehead against Katy's, startling her. "Stop telling me what to do. I'm more than capable of making a bloody cup of tea in my own home."

Katy took a step backwards, her arse hitting the wall behind her. "I didn't mean to cause any offence, I was merely trying to help."

Charlie moved forward into Katy's peripheral vision, getting ready to pounce on the woman if she took a swipe at Katy.

"Well, don't. I can make my *own* drinks in my *own* house. You can sod off, leave me alone now."

"If that's really what you want, Mrs Dodds."

"It is. No, it's not. Oh, I don't know. My damn head is so frigging muddled. I have all these questions flying around and yet I'm having trouble forming the words. Why? Why my boy?"

Katy was at a loss how to comfort the volatile woman. She knew she must, but how, without her snapping again?

"Let me make you that drink. You can go in the lounge, think about what you need to ask, and we'll go from there, how's that?"

Mrs Dodds closed her eyes. Tears seeped from the corners, and she mumbled, "I don't know what to do for the best. How to react. He's dead and he's never going to come home again. How will I cope?"

"You will, eventually," Katy said, her tone gentle.

Mrs Dodds turned and headed into the first room she came to.

"I'll make the drink," Charlie said. "I feel like a spare prick at a wedding here."

Katy smiled. "Thanks, partner. I'll go and sit with her."

"I'll poke my head in and ask her what she takes. Hopefully she won't bite it off."

Katy entered the lounge. Mrs Dodds was curled up in a ball on one end of the corner couch. "Tea or coffee?"

"Coffee, the stronger the better, with two sugars... thanks."

Charlie nodded and set off up the hallway.

Katy hesitated a second or two and then sat on the other end of the couch. "What questions do you have for me? I'll try to answer them, if I can."

The woman removed her jacket, sniffed and wiped her nose on the sleeve of her jumper. "I wouldn't know where to begin. All these questions going round my head, stupid, dumb questions that I'm too scared to voice out loud."

"No question is a silly one, not to me. You're entitled to know how your son died. All I can tell you at this preliminary stage is that his body was found tied to the tracks, two legs and one arm, the other arm was lying on his chest. If that sounds weird to you, then yes, it was the same for me."

"Who found him? Did the train hit him?"

"His legs were crushed, so we believe the train struck him. I'm sorry."

"What are you doing to catch this person? Is it the same person who killed those two girls?"

"We're unsure of the facts right now. The pathologist and Scenes of Crimes Officers are at the location now, doing their very best to find some evidence or DNA from the suspect that we might be able to use to convict this person."

"And if they've been clever and not left anything? What then?"

"We keep digging."

"Why do you believe my son was targeted?"

Katy shook her head. "We've yet to uncover a motive to any of the murders. All three crimes were set up to look like the students might have ended their own lives."

"No way, Tyler would never commit suicide, *never*. He loved his family, we meant the world to him and vice versa, he would never have put us through such heartache, not intentionally. Why would someone do this?"

"Sometimes it's the thrill of a kill that gets the person going. The thought of winding up the police, toying with us, that gives them the edge."

"That's sick. Taking someone's life, a treasured family member, just to obtain a cheap thrill. What is wrong with people?"

"It's hard to comprehend at times, I can assure you."

Charlie entered the room carrying a single mug and gave it to Mrs Dodds.

"Didn't you want one?" she asked.

Katy shook her head. "No, don't worry about us, we're fine. Perhaps you can tell me when you saw Tyler last?"

"It was last night, at around ten. He was going to bed, told me he had to get up early as he had an assignment to finish and was going to do that at the library on campus. I heard him moving around the house at around seven this morning but I drifted back off to sleep. So if your next question is going to be what time did he leave, I can't tell you."

"Don't worry, the time frame is good enough. At least we know he was here last night and the incident took place this morning. Did he mention if he was meeting anyone?"

"I think he said that Boris and Heidi were planning on going as well, but I might be wrong about that. It's possible, I've been asleep since then."

"I see. That's interesting."

"Is it, why?"

"Because Heidi and Boris are both out of reach this morning."

"You've tried to contact them?"

"After we found Tyler's body, we nipped back to the university to gather the rest of the group together."

"You did, why?"

"It's become obvious that the group are now being targeted, and it's our priority to keep the rest of the students safe."

"But that didn't occur to you to do it yesterday, when my son was still alive?"

"No, I'm sorry, it didn't. We're organising a safe house for their protection as we speak."

"Good for them. Their parents must be so grateful." Mrs Dodds' sarcasm wasn't lost on Katy.

"I'm sorry you feel that I have let you down. I can assure you that my team and I have been busting a gut during this investigation."

Mrs Dodds chose not to answer and instead blew on her coffee and then took a sip. "So, what now?"

"Tyler's body will be transferred to the mortuary where a

post-mortem will be performed either today or tomorrow. This will give us the answers we need as to how he actually died."

"He's dead, what does it matter either way?"

"It does. There will have to be comparisons made with the other two deaths. Hopefully something significant will show up that will lead us to the person responsible."

Mrs Dodds gasped. "My husband… If I don't tell him he's going to hit the roof when he gets home."

Katy wasn't sure if making contact with someone while they were on the road was such a bright idea. "I might be speaking out of turn here, but do you think it would be wise telling him if he's out there, driving?"

Her gaze drifted to a family photo, of her, Tyler and a large balding man, having a snow fight. "Maybe you're right, but I'm scared how he'll react if I don't tell him."

"Perhaps you can voice your concerns with Jill when she arrives. I'm assuming she knows your husband well enough to be aware of what his reaction might be."

"Yeah, she does. She hates him. He's not the most patient man in the world. His job is very stressful, being on the UK roads all day long, it's enough to drive the sanest of people round the twist."

Katy nodded. "I agree. Are you telling me your husband has a vile temper?"

"He's been known to fly off the handle at inappropriate times, shall we say."

"That's unfortunate. It can't be much fun for you to live on eggshells day in, day out."

"I don't, not really, he's away all week and down the pub most of the weekend."

"Which only exacerbates things, I should imagine," Katy said.

"Sometimes. He never used to be like it. It's only recently that he's turned nasty."

"Any specific reason?"

"If there is, he's always refused to tell me. I'm happy enough, I leave him to it at the weekends and put the flags out when he gets on the road again, come Monday morning."

Her words pulled at Katy's heartstrings, and it explained her overreaction when Katy had revealed that Tyler had lost his life. What did she have to live for now that he was gone? Was the husband likely to blame her for their son's death? Was Katy guilty of overthinking things after hearing this snippet? Either way, she still felt it would be foolish to break the news to a father over the phone that his only son was dead.

The doorbell rang, and Charlie offered to answer it. A woman with green and blue stripes in her greying hair flew into the room and plonked herself down on the seat next to Mrs Dodds.

"Oh, Jill." Mrs Dodds' arms flew around her sister and hugged her tightly. "What am I going to do without Tyler?"

"There, there, love. Can you tell me how he died?"

"The inspector can do that. I'm far too upset to think about it."

"Hi, Jill, I'm DI Katy Foster, and this is my partner, DS Charlie Simpkins."

"I don't care who you are, just tell me."

Here we go again! Why can't people talk civilly these days to a copper? "Of course. We were called to a major accident scene this morning and discovered Tyler had been hit by a train."

"What? How is that even possible with the security procedures in place along the tracks these days?"

"Yes, she's right, I never thought about that," Mrs Dodds added, still clinging to her sister.

"We've yet to discover the ins and outs of the crime. Forensics and the pathologist are currently at the scene."

"Did he jump in front of a train?" Jill asked.

"No, some bastard tied him to the track and a train hit him," Mrs Dodds told her, fresh tears tumbling onto her cheeks. "Why Tyler? He's never hurt a single person in his entire life, why him?"

"That's right, love. He had such a beautiful soul. I'm struggling to take this all in."

"You're not the only one... I've got to break the news to Greg yet."

"Christ, I don't envy you, Mo. He's going to go apeshit, and the wazzock will probably take it out on you."

"Don't say that. How the heck am I going to tell him?" Mrs Dodds asked her sister.

"I can be here with you when you decide to break the news," Katy interjected.

"You'd do that for me, for us?" Mrs Dodds asked, her mouth hanging open.

"Of course I would. You're never alone at a time like this, never."

"Good, because he's a force to be reckoned with, that one," Jill said.

"Don't start, Jill. I know he has his faults, but deep down he's a good man."

"Deep down, what, six feet under, where he should be? No woman should have to put up with being treated the way he treats you."

"Please, ladies, don't let the conversation deteriorate into a verbal attack on Mr Dodds, that's not going to help anyone in the circumstances, is it?" Katy shifted in her seat as both women's heads shot round to look at her.

"It makes me feel better," Jill snapped. "She shouldn't be

with him, but she knows my views on the subject, and here she is, the first sign of trouble, she knows who to call."

Mo Dodds chewed her lip. "Bloody charming, that is. Ruddy listen to yourself, first sign of trouble," she mimicked, "I've just lost my one and only son."

Jill recognised her mistake and placed an arm around her sister's shoulders. "Sorry, you know how pissed off I get when Greg's name is mentioned. It's only because I care. You deserve so much better than him. Maybe one day you'll take a step back and listen to my advice about that dreadful human being."

Mo Dodds closed her eyes. "Give it a rest, Jill."

Katy coughed to clear her throat. "I think that would be for the best. Would it be all right if we left now? We'll stay if you want us to, but the sooner we get out there and start looking for the suspect the better."

"No, you go. She'll be fine with me," Jill replied.

"Will I? You can bugger off and leave me alone if you start on about Greg again."

"I won't, I promise."

Katy and Charlie left them to it and returned to their vehicle.

"That's unusual for you," Charlie said as they eased into the car.

"What was?"

"You, making a quick getaway, after delivering the news."

"I know, I feel awful about that as well, but our priority needs to be with finding the two missing students, plus getting the new investigation into Tyler's death underway."

"Where to first? Do we visit the parents of the missing kids and get them all worked up? Or do we visit Danny's and Lizzie's parents just in case Roberts comes up with the goods and we need to whisk them away to the safe house?"

Katy chewed the inside of her cheek, contemplating

which option to choose. "Let's go with the choice that is going to give us less angst."

Charlie flicked her notebook open. "Okay, Danny's parents or Lizzie's first?"

"Which house is closer? That's providing they're at home."

"Danny's by a short distance. You want forty-five Long Larton Road."

"Can you put the postcode in the satnav for me? I'll turn the car round, I'm sure it's in the opposite direction."

"It is." Charlie got to work, and the screen lit up with a five-and-a-half-minute journey time.

"That's not too bad." Katy pulled out at the next junction and took a left into the heavy traffic.

"You were saying?" Charlie laughed. "Umm... it's an emergency by the way."

Katy grinned and hit the siren. Charlie slapped the blue light on the dashboard, and the cars that were able to move over allowed them through.

"Oh no, now you're in trouble." Charlie held up Katy's ringing mobile, and Sean Roberts' name filled the tiny screen.

"Shit! I'll kill the siren but leave the lights going." Then she motioned for Charlie to answer the phone and put it on speaker. "Hello, sir. Any luck?"

"Yes, I've managed to secure a four-bedroomed house about three miles from the station."

"That's amazing. Charlie and I are on our way to advise the parents of our plan now. Hopefully they'll agree to it without kicking up much of a fuss."

"Do you want the address?"

"Go ahead. I have you on speaker, Charlie can jot it down for me."

"It's number six Tyndale Street. A quiet location, set at the end of a lane. I decided this would be the best option for us to consider, especially as it's only a few minutes from the station."

"You did great, sir. Where can we pick up the keys?"

"I'll meet you there. You just need to tell me when."

Cringing in her mind, Katy ran through the visits they had to make before they could go back to the university to pick up Danny and Lizzie. It would be at least three to four hours' work ahead of them.

"Are you still there, Inspector?"

"Yes, sir. We're not going to be able to get there for at least three to four hours. We've got numerous visits to make to the parents. Some of those visits are going to be filled with emotion, if not all of them."

"I understand. Putting your kids in a safe house isn't for the faint-hearted, but if you can explain it's the best for all concerned, then I can't see why the parents would give you grief about it."

"Sorry, I should have told you, two of the students have gone missing."

The sound of something hitting his desk made Katy jump.

"What? Missing, since when?"

"Since a few hours ago. We have Danny and Lizzie tucked up safe in a classroom, the security guards are protecting them until we return. We've just broken the news to Tyler's mother that her son won't be coming home ever again, and now we have to share the news with Heidi's and Boris's parents that they've gone missing and aren't answering their phones."

"Jesus, can this day get any worse?"

"Not as far as I'm concerned. Well, thinking about that one, yes, I suppose it could, if we don't find Heidi and Boris soon, but I'd rather not go there, not yet."

"I'm with you on that. Let's stick to what we do know and not what could possibly happen in the future. Talking of which, didn't Lorne use to have a contact who dabbled in the unknown?"

Katy and Charlie glanced at each other, a lightbulb going off in Katy's head as Charlie reached for her phone.

"You're brilliant. We'll get on to Carol now, see if she can shed any light on what's happening."

"Glad to have been of assistance. I've got another idea I'd like to run past you as well."

Katy pulled around the car in front, and the driver beeped, annoyed. "What's that, sir?"

"To ease your burden for the day, I'm assuming the rest of your team are all indisposed, doing research at this end."

"They are, there's lots for them to go over. Go on."

"Why don't I pick up Danny and Lizzie and take them to the safe house myself?"

Katy shot Charlie an uncertain look. "I'm sure they'll be fine at the university for a few hours."

"Rubbish, I told you, I want to help you out on this case. Why don't I grab a member of your team to accompany me, if you're concerned about me getting into strife?"

Feeling the need to come up with an excuse to keep him out of the way, Katy said, "But we've already established that my team are super busy."

"One person, not all of them. I'm sure they will cope with the loss. The question is, can you? If you lost another student, how is that going to sit with your conscience?"

"Jesus, tell it as it is, sir. I feel bad enough already about Tyler losing his life."

"Damn, that wasn't my intention. I'm sorry."

"All right, I've thought about it and agree, it would be better if Danny and Lizzie were tucked up at the house ASAP. Take Graham Barlow with you, sir. I'll give him a call now, tell him what's going on."

"Good, tell him I'll drop by and pick him up in eight minutes."

Katy laughed and rolled her eyes. "Fair enough. See you later."

"And, Katy, thank you for allowing me the opportunity to become involved."

"My pleasure. I hope neither of us lives to regret the decision, sir."

He snorted and ended the call.

"Oh heck, how do you really feel about him being involved?" Charlie asked.

"No comment. No, correction, I think I'll respond to that question at the end of the investigation."

They both laughed. "He did have a cool suggestion, though."

"Giving Carol a call?"

"Yes, what do you think?"

Katy sighed and shrugged. "Let's face it, it can't do any harm. We're almost at Danny's now, maybe leave it until afterwards."

"I agree. Carol might be able to give us an indication as to where Heidi and Boris are."

"Talking of which. Ring their mobiles again, see if either of them answers. There might be a simple explanation why they haven't picked up before now, such as previously being out of range."

"Doubtful, not with the technology we have these days."

"All right, smarty-pants, it was only a suggestion. Ah, here we are. This is a nice area."

"There's a couple of cars parked on the drive, so we might be in luck."

"Yeah, we should have rung them first, eh? Always eager to get on with things, that's my problem."

They left the vehicle, and Katy rang the doorbell. A

blonde woman in her fifties answered the door a few seconds later.

"Hello, Mrs Hendricks?"

"That's right. And you are?"

"DI Katy Foster and DS Charlie Simpkins. I wondered if you would have the time to have a quick chat with us."

"Oh, I see. About what?"

"It would be better inside, away from prying ears."

"We don't get nosey neighbours around here, Inspector, and I'm not in the habit of inviting strangers into my house, whether they are police or not."

"I completely understand. It's about your son, Danny."

Mrs Hendricks gasped and slapped a hand over her gaping mouth.

Katy raised her hands. "I'm sorry, I didn't mean to alarm you. He's fine. Please, it would be better if we spoke about this inside, it's a confidential matter."

Relief filled Mrs Hendricks' features. "Please, come in. I have a friend here with me, you can speak freely in front of her. By the way, I'm Angela, and my friend is Francesca, she's the mother of Lizzie Pullman, who hangs around with my son."

"Wow, that's brilliant news. Forgive my enthusiasm, but we were going to pay Mrs Pullman a visit after we left here."

"Sounds ominous. Come through. Can I get you a drink, or will that delay you?"

"Two coffees, milk and one sugar, would be perfect, thank you."

She pointed at the first door they came to. "Go through. Wait, I'd better introduce you to Francesca first, it would be rude if I didn't." She pushed open the door. Francesca Pullman was flicking through a glossy magazine and glanced up when they entered the room. "These ladies are from the police, sorry, I'm appalling with names. They've got something to tell us about Lizzie and Danny. They were about to come and see you after they'd visited here. I'm going to make a drink. I won't be long, the kettle has just boiled. Please, take a seat. Don't start without me, will you?"

"We won't, I promise," Katy assured her.

She and Charlie took a seat on a leather couch opposite Francesca who eyed them with puzzlement. Katy introduced herself and Charlie.

"You were coming to see me as well? Did I hear that right?"

"You did."

Angela returned to the room and placed two mugs on the coffee table in front of Katy and Charlie. She sat close to Francesca, their legs touching. "What is it you have to tell us? Does this have anything to do with the unfortunate deaths of Paula and Tina?"

"In a roundabout way. I have some further news I need to share with you first. This morning, yet another member of the group was found murdered."

"No! How can this be happening?" Francesca shouted.

Angela gripped both of her friend's hands in her own. "Who? Not Danny or Lizzie, it can't be, can it?"

"No, I want to assure you that they're both safe and with the security guards at the university."

"Thank God for that, but why aren't they allowed to come home, to us?"

Katy smiled. "It's a precaution I felt I needed to make as SIO on the case. Sadly, Tyler was the one who lost his life this morning. As soon as we discovered his body, we arranged for Danny and Lizzie to be protected."

"Why are you only mentioning Danny and Lizzie, what about Boris and Heidi? You have failed to mention their names. Are they safe as well?"

"I wish I could tell you they were. Unfortunately, at the

moment they are untraceable. We have teams out there searching for them, but they're not answering their phones."

"What do you believe has happened to them?" Angela shook her head and asked.

"We're keeping an open mind for now. Our priority is to try and keep your children safe. Which is why we are here today. We've made the decision to put the children in a safe house. Which means, in order for our plan to succeed, they won't be allowed to have any access to their families."

Francesca tore her hands away from Angela's and jumped to her feet. "What? Are you insane?"

"Please, Francesca, if it means Danny and Lizzie remain safe then surely, we have to trust the police."

"Trust them? What have they done so far to save the kids? Yet another one found dead today, and you're prepared to trust them? I can't deal with this, I need to speak with my daughter, now."

Katy removed her phone from her pocket and dialled Lizzie's number. "Hi, Lizzie, how is it going there?"

"We're both fine. We're safe, that's all that matters, right? Have you found Heidi and Boris yet?"

"Not yet. I'm going to put you on speaker. I have to tell you that we're at Danny's house. We've come to tell his mum what's going on, and your mother is here as well."

"I'll put it on speaker, too. Hey, Mum, how are you?"

"Hello, darling, it's so good to hear your voice. How are you doing?"

"We're both fine. The inspector has been brilliant. I trust her and the people watching over us, Mum. Please accept what she says, she only has our best interests at heart."

"They want to take you away from us. I can't allow them to do that, Lizzie. I need you to come home. I'll protect you, you know I will. There's nothing as dangerous as a mother watching over her child. Let me do it, hon. Come home, I'll get your father to take the week off work. We'll all go away if necessary, just come home."

"I can't, Mum. The inspector knows best, not us. Three of my good friends have died this week, I can't take the risk of… well, I shouldn't have to point out what could happen if we don't trust the police. Please, Mum."

"Jesus, I feel so useless, it's a parent's job to love and protect their children, and you and the police are intent on stripping that ability away from us. Please, won't you reconsider your actions?"

"You're not being fair. We have to believe in the police, they've got this, Mum."

"Have they?" Francesca asked. "Tyler died this morning. They didn't save him, did they?"

"It's because our friends have all died that they're going to this extreme, why can't you understand that?"

"She's right," Danny added. "Mum, you're okay with this, aren't you?"

The two women stared at each other, Francesca's expression much harsher than Angela's as if pleading with her to make the right call.

"I think we should let the inspector deal with this Francesca. They're the experts, after all."

"Are you crazy? Try telling Tyler's parents that. I bet they have little trust in the police after being told their son is dead. I can't, no, I won't allow this to go ahead."

"You can't prevent it, can she?" Angela asked Katy.

"We should get the parents' permission, however, both of your children are over the age of eighteen. In the eyes of the law, they're classed as adults, they can make their own judgment in this scenario."

Francesca collapsed into the chair again and buried her head in her hands.

155

"Mum, is that you turning on the tears as usual?" Lizzie asked over the phone.

Her mother immediately stopped crying, and Angela passed her a tissue. "It's because I care about you, love."

"I know you do. Please, I don't feel safe at the moment. You have to take my feelings into consideration in all of this, don't you?"

"I know. I'm a selfish old biddy who wants to protect her child. Please don't condemn me for that, love."

"I'm not. You need to give me the freedom at some point to make a decision of my own, though. I'm calling it now. The police need to take care of us, we can't do this on our own. Please, please, don't make this harder than it needs to be, I'm begging you."

Tears pricked Katy's eyes listening to Lizzie's heartfelt pleas to her stubborn mother.

Francesca sat there, repeatedly shaking her head until finally she nodded. "Okay, I agree."

"Thank you, Mrs Pullman. It means a lot that you're willing to trust us."

"What I'm not okay with is being out of touch with her."

"We have to take the precaution, in case the killer is tracking either of their phones."

"Mum, again, it's for the best. Hopefully it won't be for long," Lizzie said in a weary voice.

"But what will I do without you in my life?"

"Consider what the option might be if the killer gets hold of me," Lizzie snapped back.

Her mother sobbed once more, and Katy tried to comfort her only for Francesca to shrug her off.

"Leave me alone. I'll never forgive you for taking her away from me, ever."

"That's your prerogative, Mrs Pullman. We all know this plan makes sense."

"Do we? I have grave doubts about that."

Angela groaned from her seat. "I think we're all aware of that by now, Francesca."

Francesca spun around and narrowed her eyes at her friend. "I can do without you turning on me."

Angela's hand flattened against her heaving chest. "I'm not. Far from it. All I'm asking is that you listen to what the children want. It's their lives in danger, not ours."

"How do we know that?" Francesca screamed at Katy, "Do you know that? That the killer won't come after us as well as the kids?"

"No, I can't be confident about that. All we can do is identify where the imminent threat lies at this stage, and that is with your children."

"So what about the families, what do you intend to do to keep us safe?"

"We would offer you advice on how to keep yourselves safe and recommend that you remain vigilant at all times."

"For how long?"

"Jesus Christ, Francesca, will you get out of the inspector's face and stop treating her as if she's the enemy here? She's doing all she can to keep our kids safe, don't keep bloody badgering her. All you're doing is delaying the inevitable. The kids want to go to the safe house, let them go. I know I'd feel relieved knowing that they're safe. Will there be protection at this house, Inspector?"

"Yes, there will be a uniformed officer on site around the clock," Katy confirmed.

"Good. Now let's get this actioned. The sooner we do that the sooner the police can get on with their job of catching the murderer."

After a significant pause, Francesca threw her arms up in the air and expelled a large breath. "All right. I'm far from happy about the situation and I know Colin is going to hit the roof, but okay, Lizzie, you have my blessing."

"Thanks, Mum. I know Dad will listen to you, if you explain the situation well enough. It makes sense all around. We'll be fine, I promise."

"Yeah, that goes for you too, Mum," Danny said. "Tell Dad not to worry or kick up a fuss. We trust the inspector to do the right thing."

Katy smiled at his words. Francesca eyed Katy with contempt.

"I've yet to see any evidence of why I should trust you, Inspector. I'm warning you now, if anything happens to my child, I'll have your head on a silver platter."

"Don't worry, it won't. Danny, you should be out of there soon. My chief inspector is on his way to pick you and Lizzie up to take you to the location."

"Thanks, Inspector. Will we see you at the house soon?"

"You will. We'll drop by later. Look after each other."

"Thank you, we will." Danny ended the call at his end.

Angela stood and hugged Francesca as they both broke down into tears.

"Have faith, ladies. You've got a good team on your side," Katy assured them and left her seat.

Charlie followed her to the door.

"I'll be in touch later," Katy said, "let you know when your children are both at the safe house."

"Thank you for all you're doing for us," Angela said.

"Yes, thank you," Francesca added, if a little reluctantly.

Katy and Charlie exited the house and jumped into the car.

Before starting the engine, Katy took a moment to reflect. "I hope we're doing the right thing here, keeping the kids away from their parents. If anything happens to them, I reckon Francesca will want to string me up from the nearest tree."

"You worry too much. Deep down you know it's the right thing to do. Want me to give Carol a call?"

"I think you should. I'll drive over to Heidi's house, see if her parents are at home."

"Or you could always ring ahead," Charlie suggested.

"Go on then, you do it while I get on the road. Carol can wait."

CHAPTER 9

"I'm sorry, who are you?"

Katy flashed her warrant card at the woman who appeared to be in a desperate hurry to leave her grand mock Georgian house on a new estate on the outskirts of Putney. "Michele Turner?"

"Yes, that's right. The police? Does this have anything to do with the break-in?"

Katy inclined her head and frowned. "What break-in?"

"Jesus, I'm on my way there now. This is an emergency, I can't hang around here if your visit is about anything else."

Katy sighed. "Sorry to inconvenience you, I promise not to detain you too long. We're really here to speak to your daughter, Heidi. Is she around?"

"No, I haven't seen her since she left for uni first thing this morning. What's this concerning?" Mrs Turner, who must have been in her fifties, glanced anxiously at her watch.

Resisting the urge to take a swipe at the woman, knowing that her daughter could be in imminent danger, Katy inhaled a breath and let it seep out slowly. "We're here because we're trying to trace your daughter."

"So you said, why?"

"We believe she could be in danger."

"How? My daughter is a martial arts expert, I have no fear for her safety. I ensured she enrolled in self-defence classes at a very young age, like any responsible parent would and should, considering girls aren't safe walking the streets alone at night nowadays."

"Are you aware of what has gone on at the university over the past couple of days?"

"Of course I am. My daughter doesn't keep secrets like that from me. We sat down and discussed the situation only last night. Why do you ask?"

"Because our investigation has turned from dealing with two murders to three."

"Oh no! Are you telling me that yet another student from the group has lost their life?"

Katy nodded. "I am. Tyler Dodds was found tied to a railway track this morning."

"Damn, poor Tyler, he was a nice lad, always very polite. He used to help Heidi with her studies now and again, if they were under pressure. Tied to the track? Oh my, I've just realised what you said, someone killed him? You mentioned three murders."

"Yes, so it would seem. Therefore, we have taken the unprecedented decision to place the rest of the group in a safe house for their protection, until the killer has been caught. That's why we're searching for Heidi. We've tried to contact her mobile several times, but it keeps going to voicemail. Can you help us? Tell us where she is likely to be?"

The colour drained from her ruddy cheeks, and she whispered, "No, I don't have a clue." Then she slid a hand into her bag and extracted her mobile. "I'll try her. My number has a special ringtone. She never ignores my calls, she knows it has to be important if I'm ringing her because my time is precious."

Katy stared at the woman, unsure how to react to such a statement. "If you wouldn't mind."

After several attempts, Mrs Turner gave up and slumped against the wall of her house. "What does this mean? Where is she?" Her eyes widened, and she launched herself off the wall again and dipped her hand into her pocket, extracted her house keys and let herself in.

Katy watched from the doorstep as Mrs Turner burst through the inner door and tore into a room at the end of the long hallway.

"Mrs Turner, is everything all right?" Tentatively, she stepped over the threshold and into the Minton-tiled hallway. She didn't have time to admire the impact of the grey-painted panelling against the stark-white bannisters and upper walls.

"No. I can't believe this is happening. It can't be."

Katy raced to the end of the hallway and poked her head into the room. She glanced back to see Charlie enter the house, an expression of grave concern on her young face.

"Michele, you have to tell me what's going on, please?"

Mrs Turner collapsed into the plush leather office chair in front of her mahogany desk in what appeared to be an office-cum-library. Her trembling hands covered her face, and she sobbed. Her head shook numerous times before she glanced up at Katy. Her tear-filled eyes pierced through Katy's soul. "I can't. I could lose everything, my job, my family, this house."

"Nothing can be as bad as that. Please, if you fear your daughter's life could be in danger, you have to tell me what the hell is going on."

Mrs Turner gulped, and fresh tears splashed onto her cheeks. "I can't. I just can't."

Katy appreciated there was only one way she was likely to change the woman's mind. She shrugged and turned her back on Michele and wandered through the house. Charlie stared at her, puzzled. Katy placed a finger to her lips and gestured for her partner to back up, to leave the property.

"Please… you can't go." Michele's voice sounded childlike, even to Katy's ears.

She swivelled to find the distraught woman clinging to the doorframe of her office, only to slide down it slowly and end up on her knees. Katy rushed back and squatted beside the distressed woman.

"What is it? You have to tell me, Mrs Turner."

"Michele, call me Michele."

"Michele, you're seriously worrying me now. I can't even begin to imagine what you're going through, but if you want my help, you're going to need to open up and confide in me."

"The key, it's missing. She must have it."

"What key?" Katy frowned and looked back to see a small cabinet door open to the side of Michele's desk.

"The key to the lab."

"Lab?"

"Where I work. Oh God, I can't do this. My daughter, I want her back, I fear for her life. You don't know what I know."

Katy gripped the top of the woman's arms and shook her gently. "Please, you're not making any sense. Tell me what the hell is going on. May I remind you that three students connected to your daughter have already lost their lives in as many days."

"I know… that's why I'm so anxious. You've got to find her. To bring her home to me, it's imperative."

"Why? Tell me what the significance is behind the missing key. What lab are you talking about?"

"I can't. It's highly classified. I would lose my job if I told you.

I have to make a call, tell my boss what has happened. I could lose everything I've strived for if this news gets out and…"

"And? You're still not making any sense. What lab are we talking about here?"

"I'm a bio-chemist. I was summoned to the lab earlier, that's where I was going when you arrived."

"Why the urgency?"

"Because my team have discovered a cabinet open and a vial of dangerous substance missing. If that gets into the wrong hands, life as we know it could come to an abrupt halt. We can't allow this to happen."

"Dangerous substance? What are we talking about here?"

"It's a form of Sarin… a nerve agent."

The words struck fear into Katy's heart. She got to her feet and immediately dialled Sean Roberts' number.

He answered right away. "DCI Roberts."

"Sir, it's DI Foster."

"Why so formal, Katy? What's going on? I'm in the car with Graham, en route to the university to collect Lizzie and Danny."

"Glad to hear it, it's crucial you get to them ASAP."

"That's my intention. You sound concerned, what's wrong?"

"I'm with Heidi's mother. She's just revealed something that, to be honest, I'm not sure how to take, sir."

"You're not making any sense, Katy. Let me pull over so I can give you my full attention."

Katy waited, tapping her foot until he came back on the line again.

"Okay, I'm back with you."

"Mrs Turner has just discovered a key to her lab has gone missing and an emergency situation has been declared."

"Christ, I'm not going to like this, am I?"

"No, sir. She's been informed that a vial of nerve agent has disappeared from the lab."

"And she thinks Heidi has taken it, is that what you're telling me?"

"She's not sure, sir." Katy took a few steps away from Michele and lowered her voice to barely above a whisper. "I'm sensing we need to get the proper authorities involved in this right away. If that vial ends up in the wrong hands... I dread to think what consequences that might have on the city of London."

"Fuck. You're right. Let me make some calls and get back to you. We'll still place Danny and Lizzie at the safe house, those plans haven't changed. If anything, I'd say the situation has become even more significant. I'll get back to you once I've made a few calls."

"I'll be here, waiting, sir." She hung up and went back to check how Michele was doing. The answer was, not very well. Katy crouched beside Michele and tried to comfort her by placing an arm around her shoulder, but the woman shrugged her off. "Please, we need to discuss this further, Michele. Are you strong enough to stand?"

Michele got onto her knees and then used the doorframe to assist herself up onto her feet.

Katy stood beside her and smiled. "That's a start. Are you up to telling me what we could be dealing with here?"

"No, I can't, it's classified information."

Katy growled. "How can you say that, knowing that your daughter and a vial of hazardous substance is missing? You have to open up to me, tell me how dangerous this situation is likely to become."

"It's a warfare weapon. In the wrong hands, millions of people could die within hours of being exposed to it."

"Jesus Christ. And you think Heidi has her hands on it?

How is that even possible? What about the security at the lab?"

Michele shrugged. "It's not been the best over the past few years due to cutbacks."

"Bollocks, that can't be right. Not when dealing with bioweapons. Shit, the devastation this could cause…"

"That's right, it doesn't bear thinking about."

"All well and good saying that, but we have to. Where would your daughter go with something like this?"

"I don't know. We have a cottage down in Cornwall, but she hates going there. I can't see her heading that way. Let me try her number again." Michele jabbed her finger at a single button on her phone and held it to her ear. "Nothing, it keeps going directly to voicemail."

"Has your daughter become unstable lately?"

"No, she's the brightest young person I know. I'm so proud of her achievements at university to date."

"I have to ask if you believe your daughter is capable of killing someone."

"No, definitely not. She hasn't got it in her." Michele's voice trailed off.

"Did you ever think she was capable of breaking into your safe and taking a key?"

"No, never. What are we going to do?"

Katy beckoned Charlie to join them. "I think we need caffeine to sustain us while we put our heads together. Can I leave that in your capable hands, Sergeant?"

"Sure. What would you like, Mrs Turner?"

"Sod the coffee, I need something far stronger than that. There's a bottle of fifteen-year-old malt in the cupboard above the kettle."

Charlie smiled and made her way into the kitchen at the end of the hallway.

"What status is the lab in?" Katy asked.

"High alert, what do you expect? Sorry, I shouldn't be snapping at you, none of this is your fault."

"It's okay, I'm used to being a punching bag for people's anguish. What are the procedures in the event of something like this occurring?"

"Everything has been put in place, again, that is classified information. What I will have to do is inform them about what we suspect has taken place. I can't believe Heidi could be driven to such lengths, what is the matter with her?"

"Has she been under a vast amount of stress lately which might have caused her to have a lapse in judgement?"

"Not that I can recall, no. Goodness me, all I can think about is the devastation this substance will likely cause in the wrong hands... I never thought for the life of me I'd ever consider my daughter to be a suspect of that ilk."

"It's okay. Try to remain calm, I'm going to need you to recount any possible conversations you may have had with your daughter that seemed odd at the time."

Michele's gaze flitted around the hallway, in every direction except Katy's. After a lengthy pause, she prompted the woman for an answer.

"Michele? Please, you can't hold back. If there's something that is coming to mind, I need to know about it, now."

"That's just it, there isn't. Don't you think I want to do everything I can to ensure this comes to an end promptly and without consequences?"

"Sorry, I didn't mean to assume otherwise. Why don't we go through to the kitchen? Take a seat in there?"

Grudgingly, she turned around and walked towards the kitchen. Charlie appeared in the doorway holding a tumbler and a mug. Michele grabbed the glass and downed half of the contents in one large gulp. Then she barged past Charlie and threw herself into a chair at the circular oak table. She cradled the glass in both hands and stared at it.

Charlie gave Katy a mug of coffee and collected her own from the counter, then the pair of them joined Michele at the table. Katy hadn't long sat down when her phone vibrated in her pocket. Excusing herself from the table, she crossed the room and answered the call.

"Ma'am, it's Karen. I've got some news on Heidi Turner."

"I'm listening. Is it good or bad?"

"A bit of both, I suppose. She's been located, unconscious in an alley close to the university. Another student found her whilst riding his bike around there."

"Bugger." Katy lowered her voice and asked, "Is she hurt?"

"The officers attending the scene reported that she had a scarf tied tightly around her neck as if someone had tried to strangle her."

"What the fuck is going on here?" Katy unlocked the back door and stepped out into a large back garden dominated by shrubs in various pots in the immediate area. Beyond, the garden was immaculately trimmed, Katy suspected by a professional gardener. "I've come outside. We're with Heidi's mother now. She's going out of her mind with worry, as you can imagine. There's the added stress of knowing that her daughter has seemingly stolen a key to the laboratory where she works. The lab contacted her to inform her that a vial of Sarin has gone missing."

"Shit! Isn't that a nerve agent?"

"Correct. Crap, you need to send a message to the scene. Everyone needs to be suited in the correct gear before going near Heidi... what am I saying, it's far too late for that, isn't it?"

"I would say so, yes, ma'am. I'll contact the hospital, tell them to treat the patient accordingly."

"Go. Do it now. The less people who come into contact with this substance the better."

"On it now, boss. If I hear any further information from the hospital, I'll give you a call back."

"Thanks, Karen. We'll monitor the situation here and then... no, wait, we're still missing Boris Connor, aren't we? That was our next port of call, to go over there and find him, take him to the safe house. We presumed he and Heidi were together."

"How strange. No, there was no one else found at the scene, ma'am. Let me do some digging at this end, ring the hospital and get back to you."

"Thanks. Chase up the alert put out on Heidi and Boris. Get Stephen to pull up any CCTV footage he can find for the area near where Heidi was found. Let's see if any of the cameras caught sight of the perpetrator."

"On it now, ma'am. I'll be in touch soon."

Katy ended the call and stood there, stretched out her neck and rotated her head in a circle until her bones cracked and the tension eased slightly. She inhaled and exhaled a couple of large breaths and then reentered the kitchen. Both Charlie and Michele turned her way. "I have some news about Heidi... they've found her."

Michele shot to her feet and flew across the room to stand in front of Katy. "Tell me she's okay. She's not dead, is she?"

Katy raised a hand to calm her. "No, she's not dead. However, I do have to warn you that she's unconscious. She was found in an alley. I'm only going by what I've been told, but it would appear that someone tried to strangle your daughter with a scarf."

Michele's eyes watered with renewed tears, and she shook her head over and over. "I knew she wouldn't be the one to have taken the vial. I mean, she might have done, but it seems likely that someone made her do it under duress, wouldn't you say?"

169

"We have no way of knowing that until we manage to speak to your daughter. Anyway, as of now, she's safe. We have another student to track down, Boris Connor. Can you make your way over to the hospital? Or do you need us to drop you off? Maybe the staff will allow you in, if you're wearing the appropriate safety clothing, what with your daughter possibly being exposed to Sarin." The hospital was miles away, and she was eager to begin the search for Boris. His home was not too far from where they were now.

"No, I'll get a taxi. Have you made the hospital aware of the predicament we are in?"

"Yes, a member of my team is getting in touch with the hospital now."

"Good. There are strict, rigorous procedures they will need to follow when they take her in. What about the vial? Did they find it?"

"My team are asking the necessary questions and will get back to me, once they obtain the answers."

Michele shuddered. "This is unbelievable. I fear how this is all going to turn out if we don't find that vial soon."

Katy was shocked that the woman's concern lay with the vial instead of with her daughter who'd had a near-death experience. "Don't concern yourself with that now, your main priority should lie with your daughter." Her tone was sharper than intended.

"Oh, yes, no, of course. I didn't mean it to sound like I wasn't putting my daughter first, I really didn't. How silly of me, what must you be thinking of me?"

"What I think doesn't really matter. You need to get to the hospital. I would suggest you make the lab aware of the developments first."

"What? Even though the substance hasn't been found?"

"Yes. They have a right to know."

"I'll do it en route to the hospital. Oh God, where did I

put my bag? I've never felt so discombobulated before. There appears to be a tornado wreaking havoc in my mind."

"I'm sure things will settle down soon. You need to be going, and so do we. We have another student's life at risk."

"Oh, my, yes. Poor Boris. I hope you find him safe and well soon. I wonder if he was with Heidi this morning."

"We won't know until either Heidi wakes up or we catch up with Boris. I just want to make sure you're going to be all right getting to the hospital."

"Yes, I have a reliable taxi service I can call upon, they've never let me down yet. I know, I'm probably treading dangerously with that statement." She went back to the table and picked up her mobile to make the call.

Katy motioned for Charlie to finish her drink and knocked back the rest of hers. She placed her empty mug in the sink and waited for Michele to end her call.

"They'll be here in ten minutes. My regular driver will then take me to the hospital."

"Great news. Okay, we're going to have to go now. If I leave you my card, will you ring me as and when your daughter wakes up? No pressure from us, but we'll obviously need to question her to find out who attacked her."

"Providing she knows, of course," Michele replied.

Katy smiled and handed over a business card, then she and Charlie left the house.

"Bloody hell," Charlie said. "What the heck is going on here? Why is the perp killing or attempting to kill off these students, and how the dickens are we supposed to arrest him with no bloody evidence or clues to go on?"

Katy picked up on the vast amount of frustration lingering in Charlie's tone. "That's where Carol comes into play, isn't it? Any luck calling her?"

They both got in the car.

"I tried, but her phone went straight to voicemail. I'll try again now."

"You do that. I'm going to take a punt and drop by Boris's home, see if we can catch either him or a member of his family in."

"I wouldn't bank on him being at home. What if he's lying in a ditch with his throat cut?"

"Ever the optimist, eh?"

"Sorry to put a downer on things, but I'm getting pretty pissed off with the body count rising daily." Charlie held up a finger to silence Katy. "Carol, hello, long time no hear." She put the phone on speaker and continued the conversation.

"There she is, I told you she would ring today, didn't I, Pete?"

Charlie gasped. "My Pete? Mum's Pete? Is he there, with you?"

"The one and only. He often pops by and has a chat with me. He's always around, Charlie, I've told you that several times in the past, it's not my fault you've chosen to ignore it. He keeps a watchful eye over you, all the time. Talking of which, he told me to pass on a message when I next spoke to you."

"Er… right, okay, and what's that?"

Katy listened with interest and noticed Charlie squirming uncomfortably in her seat. Katy snuck a sideways glance and saw the colour rise up Charlie's neck and settle in her cheeks.

"It's about your new fella, you're far too good for him. If Pete were alive today, he said he'd clip him around the ear for the way he drove out of the station car park this morning. He needs to tone it down a bit. Either that or he's going to tick off your senior officers and put your career in jeopardy."

"What? He saw that?"

"Charlie, you are naughty. I thought you were settled with Brandon," Carol said. "I was shocked when your mother told me you had parted, absolutely shocked. I know he was a bit of a limp lettuce, but I thought your love of dogs would hold you together. Bind you. Why did you split up, and who is this new chap?"

"Er... I... Sorry, Carol, I can't talk right now, not about personal stuff. You're on speaker, and Katy is in the car with me."

"Oops, hi, Katy. I wasn't aware. I hope I haven't caused anyone any embarrassment."

"Hi, Carol. No, all is good with me. Not sure Charlie would agree, though, by the colour of her cheeks."

"All right, can you two give it a rest now, please? Carol, we're in need of your expert help. Can you oblige?"

"If I can. What's up? I take it this has to do with the murder cases you're dealing with at the moment."

"Spot on, Carol," Katy said.

"Tell me what you need, and I'll see if there is anyone around who can give us a hand."

Katy allowed Charlie to continue the conversation.

"We've got three murders, all students from the local university. The thing is, they were part of a group who hung out together. There were seven in total. We've got two members on their way to a safe house with DCI Roberts, another girl has just been found unconscious, we're presuming that's an attempted murder, although it's too early to say. But the final lad, Boris, has gone missing. We're desperately trying to locate him so that we can take him to join the two remaining students at the safe house. Can you help us?"

"Let me see what I can do? Do you have time to hold on the line?"

"Yes, Katy is on the way to Boris's house now. It's our last-ditch attempt to find him."

"Okay, let me reach out, see who is around. That is, if Pete

173

will get out of my face. He's really wound up about your new fella, Charlie. He's told me to caution you to think carefully. All right, I've told her, let it drop, Pete. The girls need my help solving a mystery... I told you to leave it, now shoo, get out of my hair. Sorry about that, he's gone off in a huff. I bet he'll come back and give me hell once we're through here."

"Same old Pete. Mum says he was a worrywart, I think she used to call him." Charlie chuckled.

"And some. Right, back to business. Don't worry if the line goes quiet, I'll still be here. You know how this works, sweetie."

"I do. We'll be here, in the background, listening."

Charlie held up her crossed fingers, and Katy nodded. She drove another three miles and then pulled into Boris's road. Compared to where Heidi lived, this was a run-down area, and Katy couldn't help wondering how the students had met, coming from polar opposite backgrounds. *Don't people from different classes or backgrounds tend to stick together?*

"This is it." Katy pointed at the house with the peeling paint on the front door. One of the double-glazed windows was smashed in the top corner.

"Carol. We're going to have to leave you now. I'll give you a call later, or better still, you ring me if you come up with anything," Charlie said.

"I'll do that. I'm sorry to let you down, I'm not getting anything just now. Take care. I'll be in touch soon, I hope."

Katy and Charlie left the car and walked up the narrow path to the front door. Katy clawed the sleeve of her jacket over her knuckles and rang the bell. It tinkled once on the other side and died.

"Great." She banged on the wood instead.

Charlie took a step back and glanced at the windows above. "I think I saw some movement up there. Knock again."

Katy rolled her eyes. "Wish I'd brought my baton with

me, it would have come in handy." She knocked again, this time ensuring she pounded loudly enough to reach the person upstairs.

They waited for a few moments, and then Katy tried again. She stomped her feet to keep warm. *Open the damn door!*

After another few seconds of putting up with the icy-cold weather, the door was opened by a young man. "Boris. Gosh, are we glad to see you. We've been trying to call you for hours."

"You have? Why? My phone died last night, and I was too busy studying to put it on charge and I forgot to do it when I woke up this morning."

"Are your parents at home?"

He peered over his shoulder and pulled the door closed. "No, I mean yes, but they both work nights and are tucked up in bed. Can I help with anything?"

"We're going to need you to come with us. Can you pack a quick bag of essentials?"

"What? Why? What's going on? I don't understand. Are you arresting me? Why do I need to pack a bag?"

"Sorry, I'm guilty of being eager to keep you safe."

"Safe, from what?"

"From whom. The killer. We believe the other members of your group are in danger. Heidi Turner was found unconscious a few hours ago, and unfortunately, this morning, Tyler lost his life. Danny and Lizzie are on their way to a safe house, and we're here to take you there, to join them."

"Oh heck, my God. What the shitting hell is going on? Excuse my language. Who could be doing this? As a group, I don't think we've upset anyone, so why would someone set out to kill us all? That is what's going on, isn't it?"

"So it would seem. We're doing our very best to ensure that doesn't happen. Dean Johnson agrees with our plan. I'm sure if you're concerned about your lectures that something could be arranged, either through extra study work or maybe the lecturers will agree to you all attending via a Zoom call. I'm certain there will be a way around it."

"Where there's a will, that's Mum's motto, always has been. Can you give me five minutes to have a chat with my parents and to sort out a few necessities?"

"You go ahead. We'll wait out here in the car."

He nodded and went inside. Katy and Charlie headed back towards the car.

Katy blew out a breath. "God, it's a damn relief to have found him. I'll contact the station, call the search party off. No, you do that, and I'll ring Roberts, tell him to expect us soon."

Charlie sat inside the car, and Katy made her call outside, although she regretted her decision a few seconds into her conversation with Roberts, when the heavens opened.

"We'll be there soon. How are the others holding up?"

"They're quiet, both really upset. I'm not going to tell them about Heidi, let's keep that between us for now."

"Damn, sorry, me and my big mouth, I've already told Boris."

"Don't worry, I'm going to see how the kids are. See you, what, in half an hour or so?"

"I shouldn't think it'll take him long to shove a few things in a bag, you know what boys are like." Katy laughed and opened the driver's door to get in.

"Yeah, don't go there. TTFN."

"How did you get on?" Charlie asked.

"Roberts is staying at the house until we get there. He was as relieved as us to know that Boris was found safe and well. Let's hope we can keep it that way, eh?"

"Why the doubts? They should be fine at the house. Don't

forget they'll have an officer outside the property twenty-four-seven. Ah, here he is now."

"That's true." Katy faced the house and waved at Boris.

He gave a half-smile and jumped into the back seat, throwing his rucksack beside him.

"All set to go? Did you manage to have a word with your parents?"

"No, they were dead to the world. I thought it best not to disturb them. I scribbled a note and told them to contact you at the station. I hope I did the right thing."

"You did. I can always drop by and see them later. Our main concern is getting you to the house, safely tucked away with Lizzie and Danny."

"How are they?"

"They seem in good spirits so far. Hopefully, you guys won't be inconvenienced for too long. That's the plan anyway."

"Do you know who this maniac is?"

"Unfortunately, we don't, not at this moment, but we sense it's only a matter of time before Forensics come up with something that will lead to us capturing him."

"So you know it's a him? Why so gender specific?" Boris asked.

Katy looked at him through her rear-view mirror. "We've got CCTV footage of the perpetrator. From what we can tell, the person looks to be a male."

"You've seen his face?"

"No, the images are very grainy. However, judging by the perpetrator's build and the way he moves, I'm willing to put my neck on the line and say we're on the trail of a male."

He nodded and stared at the road ahead, as if lost in thought.

Katy concentrated on her driving, and within fifteen minutes, she drew the car to a halt outside the address of the safe house. They swiftly ushered Boris inside. Lizzie and Danny hugged him as soon as they laid eyes on him.

"Shit! Thank God you're safe," Lizzie gushed. "Have you heard how Heidi is, have you found her?" She directed her question at Katy.

"Why don't we all take a seat?" Katy pointed at the large dining table in the centre of the vast room. *This is some bloody house!*

"We're not going to like the sound of this, are we?" Danny asked.

"Don't go overthinking things," Katy warned. "You'll be pleased to know that Heidi was found about an hour ago. She's in hospital. Don't ask how she is, we haven't seen for ourselves yet. Our main aim was to get you three settled here."

Lizzie cried and then sucked in a breath as if to calm herself and said, "I don't understand any of this. Why is this happening to us? We've never wronged anyone, why?"

"I'm afraid we don't have all the answers yet, Lizzie. Now that you guys are here and safe, we can get back out there and begin the investigation once more."

"I'm glad you felt the need to protect us," Danny said. He smiled and looked embarrassed when he glanced at Katy.

Boris sat there, quietly watching what was going on around him.

"Are you all right, Boris?" Katy asked gently.

She tried to cover his hand with hers, but he yanked it away.

"Don't touch me. You should be out there, chasing this killer. It's not right that we feel threatened, unable to live our lives properly without this threat hanging over us."

"I understand how upsetting this must be for all of you," Katy said. "We're doing our best, Boris. I have to ask you all again, now that things have escalated further, do you know anyone with a likely vendetta against your group?"

The three students all stared at each other and shook their heads.

"No," Lizzie replied. "Danny and I have been sat here, trying our hardest to think of anyone, and no one has come to mind at all. I can't believe someone would come after us this way. To kill our friends, it's… unthinkable and difficult to comprehend, isn't it, Danny and Boris?"

"I should say," Danny replied.

Boris, however, still seemed deep in thought.

"Boris, is anyone coming to mind for you?"

"Nope, not at all. We're all at a loss to think who would want to hurt us, or should I say kill us, as that's obviously their intention. Can you let us know how Heidi is? Are you going to tell us what happened to her?"

"We're going to head over to the hospital now and see for ourselves. All I can tell you is that she was found close to the university. A fellow student stumbled across her. Someone had attempted to strangle her."

"Jesus, thank God they failed," Boris said.

"I agree." Lizzie shook her head. "I just find all of this so soul-destroying. As a group, all we were ever trying to do was get on with our studies. Even up on the roof, nine times out of ten we were working up there. It's inconceivable to imagine anyone having a problem with that. What gives people the right to be so angry? Angry enough to take our friends' lives?"

"I agree, it doesn't make sense," Danny said.

Roberts cleared his throat. "All we can tell you is that we've pulled out all the stops, as a Force, to keep you safe. Please hang in there. Inspector Foster and her team are exceptional at bringing criminals to justice. The killer is within our grasp now, we're closing in fast on him, faster than he realises. I want to assure you that there will be an officer outside the property at all times. And our aim is to get you back home to your families as soon as possible."

Katy nodded in agreement. "Is there anything else you need before we leave?"

The three friends either shrugged or shook their heads.

"I forgot to say, there is plenty of food in the fridge to keep you going for a few days. We'll check in with you daily, we won't dump you here and forget about you, you have my word on that," Roberts assured them.

The friends' expressions all turned serious as though the thought of them being alone scared them.

"Are you all right, Lizzie?" Katy asked, concerned.

"I'm not sure. I think so. I suppose you'd better ask me that once all this is over. I'm glad I have Danny and Boris here with me and that I'm not having to go through all this alone."

"I'm glad you've all made it this far and are together now as well. Take care. We'll be in touch soon."

"If she's awake, will you give Heidi our love and tell her we'll see her soon?" Lizzie said.

"I will, sweetheart. She's in safe hands, and so are you."

Katy, Charlie and Sean Roberts left the house together.

Katy paused at the front door to have a word with the male uniformed officer on guard for the first shift. "I'm going to give you my card. Ring me day or night if anything untoward happens that you're unsure about. These guys need to remain on the premises at all times, no matter what excuse they try and give you."

"Yes, ma'am, leave them to me. I've got a kid brother their age, so I know all the tricks they're likely to try and pull."

Katy laughed. "I bet. How long are you here for?"

"Until ten this evening, so not too long now."

Katy took a brief look at her watch. "Shit, is that the time already? Okay, take care, ring me if you need me."

"I will. Do you want me to pass your card on to the next officer who shows up?"

"Yes, do that."

She joined Charlie and Sean at her car. "Are you sure we're doing the right thing, leaving them here alone? My gut says otherwise."

"You worry too much. They'll be safe, and one of our lot will be on duty throughout their stay," Sean replied. "I'm going to head back to the station now. Thanks for giving me a buzz, allowing me to get involved today. I've loved it."

"My pleasure. Thanks for getting the house sorted so quickly. We're going to the hospital now, see what's going on over there."

"I don't suppose there's been any news on the missing vial yet, has there?" Sean asked.

"Not as far as I know. We'll give the station a call on the way."

They got in their respective cars and drew away from the detached house, situated high on a hill at the end of a quiet lane.

"This is an ideal location. Crap, I didn't realise it was so late. Almost five, and we've achieved virtually nothing all day."

Charlie laughed. "Are you kidding me? We haven't stopped all day. I'd say we've achieved a great deal but maybe I'm biased."

Katy's mouth twisted. "Er, I suppose. Either way, it's been a long day, and it hasn't finished yet."

CHAPTER 10

$\mathcal{U}$pon their arrival at the hospital, they were ushered to an area down in the basement and, as a precaution, were given special protective suits. They found Michele Turner outside a room which had a large window to one side of the door. She was staring at her daughter, who was lying in a special see-through tent. Again, every precaution was being taken into consideration to protect Heidi and the medical staff attending to her needs.

"How are you holding up?" Katy asked Michele.

"I'm all right, it's my daughter I'm worried about."

"Have the doctors told you anything about her condition yet?"

"Not really. They've informed me all her vital signs are okay, sort of. Her heart rate is slower than normal, but they said that's to be expected with what she's been through."

"Okay, it's good to see everything is in place to keep everyone protected. Any news on the missing vial yet?"

She shuffled her feet. "No, nothing as yet. I feel guilty about it being out there. Devastation abounds if that is released in the air, I can tell you. Do you think the killer intentionally attacked my daughter, forced her to steal the vial and then tried to kill her?"

"It appears to be a fair assumption. How was Heidi able to get into the lab in the first place?"

"I don't know. All I can assume is that the staff let her in, thinking that she was paying me a visit, which she often does."

"Ah, that explains it. Maybe after this incident, you might want to take another look at the security you have in place over there."

"Don't worry, we will. If I still have a job after this calamitous episode hits the news."

"Mistakes happen in all walks of life. I'm sure your bosses will go easy on you in the circumstances."

"I wouldn't if the boot was on the other foot. What about the other students? Are the rest of them safe now?"

"Yes, we managed to locate Boris, and he's joined Lizzie and Danny at the safe house. We dropped Boris off and thought we'd pop in on our way back to the station."

"I'm so relieved to hear that they're okay. I've been going out of my mind with worry, not just for my daughter but for them as well. Do you have any clues as to why the group were targeted or who by?"

"Nothing as yet. Hopefully, there will be some positive news awaiting us when we get back to the station. Knowing that the others are all safe will give us the freedom to delve into possible motives of the suspect. Has anything come to mind while you've been here?"

"I have been thinking non-stop about the situation, and no, nothing has come to mind. I suppose all the other parents have told you how good their kids are and how much they've been enjoying their time at uni, the same as I have."

"Something along those lines. It's all such a mystery to us.

We're going to leave you to it. You've got my number. Will you call me as soon as Heidi wakes up?"

"I will, well, after I've had a cuddle with her. I've come so close to losing her, I need to tell her how much I love her. Maybe I'm guilty of neglecting her lately. The mind plays strange tricks on you when guilt deals a hand."

"You shouldn't punish yourself, none of this was your fault. I know it's difficult right now, but try to remain positive about Heidi, she looks like a fighter to me."

"She always has been. Even as a baby, she was born premature and the doctor gave her a couple of months to live at the most. They didn't know what was wrong with her. It took them three years to finally give us a proper diagnosis. She had a disease that attacked the nervous system that is so rare, only one in a million people have it. For the life of me, with my head so messed up, I can't recall what it was. Anyway, once she reached puberty, her body righted itself, and she developed into a thriving teenager."

"Triumph over adversity, there, I told you she was a fighter. Stay strong. Is your husband aware of the situation?"

"He's not, not yet. He's away at a business conference. I didn't want to bother him, not until I had some good news to share with him. You know what it's like, women need to manage their relationships with certain types of men. My husband is one of those."

"I completely understand. We'll be in touch soon."

"Thank you for all you've done so far, Inspector. I know this week can't have been easy for you and your team."

"It hasn't been, but we're always up for a challenge."

Katy and Charlie said their farewells and left the hospital.

On their way back to the station, Katy's mobile rang. "DI Foster."

"Ma'am, it's me, Stephen. I've got some news and, er... it's going to throw the investigation into a major spin."

Katy rolled her eyes at Charlie. If there was ever a member of the team who liked nothing better than to exaggerate at times, it was Stephen. "I'll be the judge of that. What's up?"

"When I got back to the station with DCI Roberts, I started trawling through the CCTV footage from around the tracks where Tyler was found this morning."

Katy's heart raced. *Oh God, let this be it! The evidence we need to bring this bastard down, so these kids can get back to living their normal lives ASAP.* "Go on, Stephen."

"I managed to catch someone lingering down by the tracks. When I compared the photos from the other two crime scenes, I'm prepared to put my job on the line and say they're the same person. Same clothes, the walk is the same, their posture, everything."

"That's great news. Not that there was any doubt." Katy's attention was drawn to Charlie answering her own mobile. She half-listened to the conversation.

"Carol, hi... what...? How sure are you...? I'm sorry to doubt you, I didn't mean to do that. Jesus, okay, we'll shoot over there now... We'll let you know... I hope it's not too late."

Katy's gaze drifted from the road to her partner more times than if she were watching a match-winning set at Wimbledon.

"Sorry, Stephen, I was a bit distracted. What did you say?"

"It's Boris!" Stephen replied anxiously.

"What is?" Katy asked, confused.

"He's the killer," Charlie said. "Carol has confirmed it. We need to get back to the house now."

The car skidded to a halt, and Katy and Charlie both catapulted towards the dashboard.

"Fuck, fuck, fuck. There's been something about him that

185

has niggled me from the get-go." Katy spun the car around and hit the siren.

Charlie flicked the switch to put the lights on.

"Stephen, are you still with us?" Katy asked.

"Yes, ma'am. What do you need me to do?"

"I need the team, all of you, except one manning the phones, to get over to the house. Sign out Tasers, go prepared. We're on our way back there now. Use your sirens, but switch them off well in advance. The last thing we need is to alert him of our arrival."

"I'm on it, boss. We'll see you there."

Katy disconnected the call and heaved out a large sigh. Weaving her way through the traffic, she shook her head and intermittently thumped the steering wheel. "We had him in the damn car with us. The fucking little shit has played us like fools the last few days. Had us running around like headless chickens going here, there and everywhere, and all the time he's been laughing at us."

"You're going to need to calm down, Katy, if you want to get us there in one piece," Charlie advised.

"What did Carol say? How does she know it's him?"

"One of the girls came through to her, it was Paula. She told Carol that it came as a shock to her that Boris pushed her off the roof. They had always got on well together, and then he turned on her."

"Why? What's going on in that head of his?" Katy fell silent, and her mind swirled with different scenarios. The one that was most prominent had her reaching for her phone.

"Don't do that. Let me call whoever you're intending to contact, you need to concentrate on your driving."

"All right, you win. Call Roberts for me. He needs to be in on this. My life won't be worth living if I don't involve him after what he did for us today. Put it on speaker."

Charlie scrolled through Katy's recent contact numbers and jabbed at the chief's.

The phone rang a couple of times, and then Roberts said, "Katy, is that you?"

"Sir, sorry to trouble you."

"Wait, why are you using your siren? What's going on?"

"It's all kicked off. We know who the damn killer is, and he's at the safe house."

"What? How is that possible?"

"He's one of them. Boris is the bloody killer. I need you to organise an Armed Response Team to meet us at the location."

"Leave it with me, I'll do it en route. See you there." He ended the call before Katy had the chance to object.

"I knew what his reaction would be. Oh shit!"

"What are you thinking?"

"The vial!"

"The vile what? Oh crap, forget I said that. Doh! You think he's got the nerve agent?"

"Don't you? It seems feasible, if Heidi had it in her possession and he tried to kill her. Maybe that's where he slipped up. He thought he'd killed her instead of leaving her for dead down that alley, not thinking that someone would come along and save her. Shit. Get Roberts on the phone again."

Charlie called the number.

Roberts answered on the first ring. "Jesus, woman, give me a chance to organise things, for fuck's sake. What now?"

"Something has just occurred to me, sir, that needs to be dealt with before we go in there."

"What's that?"

"I reckon he's got access to the nerve agent."

"Fuck! Holy shit. This could be... no, I'd rather not go there. Leave it with me. I'll make the necessary calls and get the ball rolling. I'll see you at the house."

Katy ended the call and then slammed her fist onto the steering wheel once more. "I'm so tempted to call either Lizzie or Danny."

"No, you can't risk it. If you tell them Boris is the killer, it's only going to put the poor buggers in a spin. He'll be thinking up ways to kill them, let's use that to our advantage."

"How? I'm not with you."

"Every time he's committed a murder, he's set it up as a suicide. With two students in the house, it's going to be tricky for him to get away with that."

"You're forgetting one thing... the nerve agent. He could take them both out with that... and himself, if that's his intention."

"Yes, his endgame. To kill all the group and then himself. What about his parents? We should let them know what's going on. Maybe they'll be able to talk him around for us."

"It's worth a chance. Make the call, Charlie."

Charlie ended the unsuccessful call moments later with a sigh of her own. "No answer. Why am I not surprised?"

"When we picked Boris up earlier, didn't he say his parents were in bed after being on the night shift? Do people sleep that long, even when their shift pattern is different to what normal people tend to do?"

"Hmm... it was around four when we were at his house earlier. Maybe they sleep until four-thirty or five. I suppose it depends on what time they got to bed. Want me to send uniform round there to try and rouse them?"

"Yes, do it." Katy indicated and overtook a slow car at the next junction. A blast of the horn from a car coming in the other direction made her curse under her breath. "Fecking idiot, he could see and hear us coming. What is wrong with people?"

Charlie chuckled. "You're so funny when you're vexed."

"Glad I amuse you." She glanced in her rear-view mirror and saw another two sets of flashing lights behind them. "Looks like the troops have arrived. We can't be that far away from the house now. Let's cut the blues and twos."

Charlie switched off the lights and the siren, and silence reigned in the car once more. "That's better. I don't think my ears will ever get used to that din."

Katy smiled. "What it must be like to have A1 hearing, I think mine's on the blink already. Getting old is no picnic."

"Jeez, I've heard it all now. Don't let Mum ever hear you talk that way. She's what? Fifteen years older than you and rarely goes on about her age."

"I know. She's in a class of her own, though."

"If you say so."

Katy was relieved to see the cars following had turned off their lights and sirens as well. She turned into the road and drew to a halt a fair distance from the house. It was lit up like Blackpool at Christmas.

"Bloody kids, they have no idea how much electricity costs these days," Katy grumbled.

"Er... I'd say that's the least of their worries at the moment. What's that?" Charlie pointed ahead of them.

Two figures emerged from the house, both male, one chasing the other.

"Fuck, we need to get after them." Katy started the engine and flicked on the siren, alerting the two youths they were there, watching the proceedings. The figures dipped over the brow of the hill and out of sight. Katy put her foot down and drove after them. She paused outside the house and let Charlie out of the car. "Tell one car to follow me and the other to stay with you. Be careful, Charlie. You know the risks."

"Don't worry. Just get the bastard."

Katy drove after the figures a short distance until the

189

lane ran out. The boys headed through a farm gate towards the wooded area up ahead. "Shit, there's no way I can risk going after them now." She slammed on the brakes and got out of the car to speak to the officers following her. It had been hard to make out who they were in the dark. "Patrick, glad you're here. You, too, Graham. Two figures, I'm presuming they were Boris and Danny, left the house as we showed up and ran into the woods. Here's the thing, they could be armed with a nerve agent, the one Heidi possibly stole from her mother's lab. DCI Roberts is organising an ART to join us at the house. I'm not sure what to do, send you after them or to let them go and wait for the backup to arrive."

"If you don't mind me making a suggestion, ma'am," Patrick said. He peered over his steering wheel for a better look in the dark.

"You know you can speak freely. What's on your mind?"

"Why don't Graham and I stick with them, on foot for now? That way we'll be able to give their location when the backup team arrives."

"It's the nerve agent aspect that's throwing me in a spin. If the bastard releases it into the air, it'll spread rapidly. There's no telling how many people will be affected then."

Graham shrugged. "It's got to be a risk we're going to have to take, ma'am. What's the alternative? That he kills the other student and goes on the run again? We've come this close, it would be foolish for us to back down now."

Katy sucked in a large breath. "Go, stick with them. Keep in touch at all times. I need to get back to the house, see what's going on there. Thanks, guys."

They ditched the car and set off on foot, vaulting the gate as Katy hopped back into the driver's seat and turned the car around. She braked outside the house and tore through the front door, pausing to stare down at the dead officer lying on the doorstep whose throat had been cut. *Shit! I need to deal with this later.* "Charlie, where are you?"

"Help, I'm upstairs, Katy. Help me, she's dying."

Katy bolted up the stairs, two at a time. "Where are you?"

"In the end bedroom. Hurry."

The hallway seemed to go on forever. Eventually, Katy reached the bedroom she was after and flew across the deep-pile carpet towards Charlie and Lizzie, who was lying on the floor in front of her.

"I can't find a pulse. God, I've tried and I can't find one," Charlie shouted, distraught.

Katy tugged at her arm and sent Charlie off balance so she could gain clear access to Lizzie's body. She loosened the clothing around Lizzie's neck and placed her fingers on her flesh.

"Christ, it's there, faint, but there is a slight one. Have you called for an ambulance?"

"I didn't have the time. Thank God she's still alive. I'll do it now."

Charlie removed her phone from her pocket and rang nine-nine-nine. Katy listened to her giving the operator their location while she tried to make Lizzie more comfortable.

"Lizzie, can you hear me? Lizzie, please come back to us, sweetheart. Don't you dare give up on us now."

She noticed Lizzie's right hand twitch and swept a few stray hairs away from the teenager's face.

"You're going to be all right, the ambulance is on its way. We're here with you. You're safe, you're going to be fine."

Lizzie's eyes flickered open, and she gasped for breath.

Katy hoisted the youngster's upper torso onto her lap. "Take your time. Breathe deeply but slowly. Are you all right?"

"Danny... where's Danny?"

"It's okay. We saw them as we arrived. My team are out

there, chasing after them. Can you tell us what happened?"
Katy's gaze took in the room. There was a rope hanging from one of the beams.

"He tried to kill me. Boris. It was him all along. I dread to think what would have happened if Danny hadn't heard me cry out and come to see what was going on. Boris knocked me out cold. I can't tell you what went on after that."

"It's okay. You're still with us, that's all that matters. I'm sorry we put you through this. We had no idea Boris was the killer, not until about twenty minutes ago. We came back as soon as we figured it out."

"It's okay. You can't let him get away with this."

"We won't, I assure you. Did he have the vial with him?"

A frown pinched Lizzie's brow. "What vial? I didn't see one."

"That's a relief. We believe he somehow got Heidi to steal a sample of nerve agent from her mother's laboratory."

"Oh God, no. How is Heidi, do you know?"

"She's being well cared for. Don't worry about her. Ah, I can hear the ambulance coming now. They'll whisk you off to hospital, out of harm's way."

"I asked him why he was persecuting us and why he'd killed the others. He just grinned at me and said because he could. That look he gave me, it chilled me to the bone. He's nothing but a monster, and to think we brought him into our group because we felt sorry for him."

"Sorry for him? May I ask why?"

"He told us his parents had recently died and he was all alone in the world now. We took pity on him, I suppose. The boys were against us inviting him to join us; we should have listened to them. None of this would have happened if we had."

"You can't blame yourselves for being decent people, Lizzie. As I told Heidi's mother earlier, none of this is her fault, and it's not yours either. You reached out to a person in need, and it backfired."

"Backfired? That's one way of putting it." Lizzie forced out a smile and then closed her eyes as if the exertion to tell Katy what had taken place had been too much for her.

Katy reached for a pillow from the bed and placed it under Lizzie's head then squeezed out from underneath her. "I'll be back with the paramedics, stay there."

At the door, Katy stared back at Lizzie and said to Charlie, "Boris told her that his parents were dead."

"Crap, really? Well, I guess we'll know soon enough. Want me to go downstairs and let the paramedics in?"

"Yes, do that. I'm going to have a quick scout around up here, see what I can find."

Charlie thundered down the stairs, and Katy nipped next door to a bedroom the same size as Lizzie's. She searched the rucksack on the bed, recognising it to be Boris's. Carefully, she slid her fingers into every pocket and gasped when she touched something cold in the last one she checked at the rear of the bag.

"Shit! I think this is it."

"What is it?" a masculine voice said from behind.

"Bloody hell, you scared the crap out of me, sir. I think I've located the vial."

"Okay, leave it where it is, we'll let the experts deal with it. Let's go downstairs. The ART and the lab folks should be here soon."

"I'd rather stay with Lizzie. She's in the other bedroom."

"No need. The paramedics are with her now. Come on, Katy, we need to do some strategizing. Where's Boris?"

"Patrick and Graham are in hot pursuit of him and Danny through the woods at the end of the road. I need to contact them, tell them we've found the vial and to take Boris down at the earliest opportunity."

"Good idea. I'll make the ART commander aware of the situation, see what he suggests we do next."

THE NEXT HALF an hour was hectic on all fronts. Lizzie was placed in the ambulance and taken to the hospital. The lab techs identified the danger with the vial and secured it in a large metal capsule. Katy, Charlie and Sean Roberts all made their way down to the woods along with the ART. A lot of shouting went on amongst the trees until Boris and Danny emerged with Patrick and Graham holding each of their arms, armed men accompanying them, until Boris was secured in the back of Patrick's vehicle.

"Thank God for that," Katy whispered, her shoulders slumping through sheer exhaustion.

Sean squeezed her forearm. "Another investigation drawn to a satisfactory conclusion, DI Foster. Congratulations."

Katy grimaced. "Why don't I feel like celebrating?"

"You will, eventually." Sean placed an arm around her shoulders and pulled her against his chest.

Tears welled up, and she swallowed the lump in her throat. "It's been one of the worst weeks in my life. I feel as though we've let the families down as well as the students who never made it. Plus, not forgetting we lost one of our own tonight, too."

"Stop it, Katy. You did your best, we all did," Charlie said.

"Listen to your wise partner, she knows best. I'll deal with losing the constable and all that entails," Sean said, giving her another hug.

Katy's mobile rang, and she swiftly withdrew it from her coat pocket to answer it. "DI Katy Foster."

"Ma'am, it's Constable Willow. I was told to come to the Connors' address. Sorry to have to inform you that we've found two dead bodies at the location."

"Shit! Can you identify them?"

"Yes, we've got ID in the form of two driving licenses belonging to Rebecca and Leo Connor."

"Thanks, those are the boy's parents. We've arrested him, he's on his way to the station. Can you do the necessary there, secure the crime scene and call the pathologist? Wait, how did they both die?"

"Their throats have been cut, ma'am."

"Callous fucking little shit. Thanks, Constable."

"Yes, ma'am. Leave things to me."

She ended the call and tipped her head back to look at the clear black sky. "It takes a deranged soul to want to slit their own parents' throats."

"He didn't?" Charlie said, shocked.

"Yep, it shouldn't surprise me, he's one hell of a troubled teenager. I'm so glad we caught him before he had a chance to do something with that vial." Her phone rang again. "DI Foster, how can I help?"

"Katy, sorry, DI Foster, it's Michele Turner."

At the sound of Mrs Turner's voice, Katy's heart sank. "Hello, Michele. Is everything all right?"

"Yes, it couldn't be better. My daughter has regained consciousness. She revealed something shocking that I wanted to tell you about right away."

"What's that?" Katy found herself reaching for Charlie's hand and closing her eyes.

Charlie squeezed her hand in return.

"Heidi told me the person who tried to kill her was Boris Connor."

Katy's eyes opened, and she released Charlie's hand with a smile. "We know. Don't worry, we have him in custody."

"You do? Thank goodness, that's wonderful news. Dare I ask about the vial?"

"It's safe. It's on its way back to the lab now."

"Oh, my days. I'm so relieved. It's turned out to be a good day after all."

"You could say that. I'm going to have to go. I have a suspect to question back at the station. Give my best wishes to your daughter. I'll be in touch soon. We'll need to take a statement from her in a few days, when she's better."

"Don't worry, we've already discussed that. I can't thank you enough for all you've done. Congratulations on capturing Boris."

"Thanks, everything came together at the right time, for a change. You take care of yourself and Heidi."

EPILOGUE

*B*oris sat opposite Katy and Charlie in the interview room, defiance lingering in his cold green eyes. "No comment."

Katy glanced at the duty solicitor who shrugged and then looked down at her notes.

"No comments are not going to help you, Boris, not when the evidence is stacked against you."

"What evidence?"

"The evidence Lizzie, Danny and Heidi are willing to reveal in court. Then we have the hair samples we found on Tyler's body—a few dyed red hairs, they're pretty distinctive in colour. We also have your fingerprints on the rope used to bind Tyler's limbs to the track."

He grinned.

Katy continued, even though she was tempted to reach across the table and throttle the smug bastard. "We've also got the weapon used to kill both your parents and the officer standing guard outside the safe house."

"Not so safe after all, was it?" He laughed.

Katy seethed. She hated it when serial killers mocked her,

especially when they were Boris's age. "So, are you going to tell us why? Why you chose to infiltrate the group and kill them?"

"Let's see now. Where do I begin?"

Her eyes narrowed, and she wondered if he was toying with her again, or if this time, he was going to tell the truth instead of going down the customary 'no comment' route.

He paused, testing her willingness to remain calm. Eventually, he held up a hand and pressed each digit as he reeled off why each student was attacked.

"My father turned out to be a useless C-U-N-T. His business suffered during the pandemic; he knew the parents of the other students."

"In what capacity?"

"My father had a heart attack, through the stress of dealing with his business that was in decline. The parents of the other group members did nothing to prevent him from going under. We had it all, lived in a large house, close to Michele Turner, up until last year, when the money dried up and my father's health deteriorated even more, then we were forced to live in that hovel, because we couldn't afford to live anywhere else."

"How were the students' parents to blame for your father's downfall? I'm struggling to figure that out."

He held his right hand up and prodded the first finger. "The bank manager, Lesley Falkirk, refused to loan him the money he needed to get the business back on track."

"Paula's father, right?"

"Correct. Susan and Terrence Webster are money-grabbing fuckers. Two years ago, at the start of the pandemic, they came cap in hand to my father, asking him to invest in their boat business, only to see those deals fold before they got off the ground."

"So you punished their daughter, Tina, for the parents' sins?"

"Correct. Michele Turner promised my father she would help to raise some funds for him. He was banking on that money to keep the roof over our heads, only for Michele to go back on the deal. She conned him, all because she wanted our house."

"What? She lives in your house?"

"No, her sister does. Conniving fucking bitch. She led my father up the garden path and ended up throwing him on the compost heap."

"Okay, so what about Tyler? Where do his parents fit into all of this?"

"They don't. He was just there. He suspected I was the killer, started bombarding me with questions. He had to go. He was hampering my mission."

"What was your endgame, Boris? Why did you kill your parents?"

"Because they let me down. We had it all and then we ended up with nothing. The rest of the group treated me with sympathy. At first, I was grateful, and then it started to wind me up. I didn't want their fucking sympathy. Their parents should have stepped up to the plate to help my parents when they needed it the most."

"So you took your revenge and killed three innocent students?"

"That's right. Their parents needed to be taught a lesson. They needed to learn that they couldn't treat me like shit after what they'd done to my father."

"But to kill your own parents just because their business failed due to the most debilitating times in our recent history is, well… bizarre and nonsensical."

"Answer me this, Inspector, have you ever had everything

you ever wanted only to lose it all... through no fault of your own?"

"No, however, we're living through unprecedented times, and when they hit, the likelihood of someone being affected the way your parents were becomes inevitable. But most people would accept the situation rather than go out there and punish the people they believed were at fault."

He grinned. "I ain't most people, am I?"

"No, I can see that. Is there anything else you'd like to tell us?"

"Had you not caught me when you had, I would have killed Lizzie and Danny and then released the vial at King's Cross Station. There's always a crowd hanging around there."

"Why? What would you have hoped to have achieved by doing that?"

Boris shrugged. "Fuck knows, I guess it would have made me feel better, knowing that dozens, maybe hundreds of people would have lost their innocent lives all because the security at that lab was inadequate."

"And you know that Michele would have probably lost her job in the process, right?"

"Shit happens, as they say. Maybe it would make her and the others think more, force them to put others first instead of thinking only of themselves for a change."

"That's a warped mind you have there, Boris." Katy stared at him, gauging his reaction to her insult.

He smiled and bowed his head. "Why thank you. I'll take that as a compliment."

Katy's stare intensified. "Take it whichever way you like. You'll spend the rest of your life behind bars, contemplating what your future would have been like, if bitterness hadn't clouded your judgement."

"Whatever. I have no regrets."

Katy's gaze rose to the uniformed copper behind Boris. "Take him back to his cell, we're done here."

Charlie said the necessary to end the interview, and they all left the room.

Katy showed the duty solicitor to the main entrance and shook her head. "He's a cool customer."

"An evil one, you mean. I'll be glad to pass this one over to someone more senior to deal with. I'll look at it as a bonus not being fully qualified yet."

Katy smiled and shook her hand.

AFTER STOPPING off for a low-key celebratory drink at the local pub, Katy drove home to find Lily's car parked in her space. Instead of getting worked up, she brushed it aside and entered the house. "Hi, everyone, I'm home," she shouted while she removed her coat and shoes at the front door.

Georgie came running into the hallway and placed her arms around Katy's middle. She hugged her daughter back hard.

"Hi, Mummy. Daddy is in the kitchen, talking tactics with Lily."

"Ah, okay. Did you have a good day at school, sweetheart?"

"I did. I drew a monkey. Daddy told me to pin it up on the fridge."

"How exciting. You can show me, if you like?"

Georgie slipped her hand into Katy's and tugged her into the kitchen. "Daddy, Daddy, Mummy's home."

AJ grabbed his squealing daughter and wrestled with her. Once he'd finished, he glanced up and gave Katy the most loving smile imaginable. "Welcome home. Have you had a rough day?"

Katy's gaze drifted to the other side of the table. Lily had her head down, making notes in her A4 spiral-bound pad.

"I'll tell you about it later. Hi, Lily, nice to see you again."

"Oh, hi, sorry, I was otherwise engaged on our next mission."

"Good to hear."

"Lily has been in touch with a few contacts, and it would appear they're eager for us to host a dozen or more kids' parties next month."

"How wonderful. You must both be thrilled." And Katy meant it, there wasn't an ounce of jealousy in her words.

"We are." AJ beamed. "Can I fix you something to eat? I didn't realise that was the time."

Lily gasped and glanced at her watch. "Neither did I. I must be going. My fella will wonder where the heck I am."

Katy raised an eyebrow. "Have you been together long?"

"A lifetime, too long to remember," Lily admitted, the colour rising in her cheeks.

"Maybe we can arrange to all meet up one night, or at the weekend?" Katy asked.

"Sounds good to me. I'll leave you nice folks to get on with your evening. I'll go over the finer points in the morning, AJ, and I'll get back to you by lunchtime."

"If you're sure? Thanks for pulling out all the stops on this one, Lily."

She gathered her things together and flew out the door after bidding them all a good evening.

"She's good. Organises me well during the day. Not sure how I coped before she came along," AJ cautiously sang Lily's praises.

"I'm glad you found her. She seems to know her stuff. Let's hope she brings in a mountain of business for you."

"She will, I'm sure. Sit down. Do you want a glass of wine? I've got a thick piece of salmon for dinner."

"Have you eaten, poppet?" Katy asked Georgie, pulling her daughter onto her lap for an extra cuddle.

"I had scampers earlier, Mummy."

Katy frowned at AJ who was laughing. "She means scampi. I thought I'd try her on it. She loved it."

"Oh, wow, I bet that was scrummy."

"It was. My tummy loved it, Mummy. Can I get down now?"

Katy released her grip on her daughter and eased her back onto the floor. Georgie ran into the lounge and returned carrying her large doll and her teddy bear called Maurice. She sat on the rug near the table and played with them.

"It's good to see her so happy," AJ said.

"It is. This is what I needed, to come home to after a hard day at work, to see the smiles on your faces. Life's too short to be falling out with each other, AJ. I'm sorry for ever doubting you."

"You're forgiven, not that there was anything to forgive. Just remember this, I would never, not in a gazillion years, jeopardise what we have here. You guys are everything to me."

She left her chair and walked into his outstretched arms, and they shared a loving kiss then turned their gazes to Georgie, happily talking to her doll and teddy, without a care in the world.

THE END

THANK you for reading See No Evil, if you haven't read the original award-winning Justice series yet, you can pick up the first book in the series Cruel Justice here.

· · ·

HAVE you read any of my fast paced other crime thrillers yet? Why not try the first book in the DI Sara Ramsey series <u>No Right to Kill</u>

WHY NOT TRY the first book in the DI Sam Cobbs series, set in the beautiful Lake District, <u>To Die For.</u>

PERHAPS YOU'D PREFER to try one of my other police procedural series, the DI Kayli Bright series which begins with <u>The Missing Children.</u>

OR MAYBE YOU'D enjoy the DI Sally Parker series set in Norfolk, <u>Wrong Place.</u>

OR MY GRITTY police procedural starring DI Nelson set in Manchester, <u>Torn Apart.</u>

OR MAYBE YOU'D like to try one of my successful psychological thrillers <u>She's Gone</u>, <u>I KNOW THE TRUTH</u> or <u>Shattered Lives.</u>

KEEP IN TOUCH WITH M A COMLEY HERE.

Pick up a FREE novella by signing up to my newsletter today.
https://BookHip.com/WBRTGW

BookBub
www.bookbub.com/authors/m-a-comley

Blog

http://melcomley.blogspot.com

Why not join my special Facebook group to take part in monthly giveaways.

Readers' Group

Made in the USA
Coppell, TX
17 March 2023

14352124R20120